ROME IN MOONLIGHT

Rome in Moonlight

JOSEPH CHIBA

ACKNOWLEDGMENTS

I wish to express my thanks and appreciation to the following individuals for their support and guidance: Sally Kigasawa, Naoko Mitchem, Chie Fiesta and Roland Fiesta, Aki Matsuyama and Don Matsuyama, George Huang and Helen Huang, Milton Wheeler and Noelani Wheeler, Mio Shimoda Ugai and Takao Ugai, Melissa Majewski and Jeff Hamano, Misato Murayama Inabnit, Mana Ban and Kenneth Hoffman, Chie Homma and Nicholas Kodani, Keith Ito and Iris Ito, Noreen Lam, Rani Shigemitsu, Pat Jennings and Eric Jennings, Pam Fonoti, Jay Jacinth, Matt Madison, Bryan Martin, Donald DiDomenico, Kim Brisbin, Mohan Gaanz, Yuko Kumlin and Rocky Kumlin, and Luca Ansaldo and Daniela Garassi. An affectionate thank you goes to the Mastrogiulio family members from both sides of the Atlantic who have been reunited after so many years apart: Frances, William, Annamarie, Diane and Debra from New York, and Inez, Iria, and especially John and Joseph from Naples, who were responsible for jump-starting in me the idea for this story. I would also like to thank my amazing editor, Laura Apgar for working so hard on this project and for helping me express the messages of love and hope I've tried to convey in this book. A heartfelt thank you must also go to my incredibly talented designer, Danna Mathias for capturing the essence of the romantic city of Rome in the perfect light. And finally, a special thanks to the extraordinary woman who has touched my life, and taught me that taking chances when you're scared brings you face to face with this exhilarating thing we call life. My wife, Sakura – the most positive and supportive woman I have ever known.

*To all the lovers around the world, old and new,
who find love every day*

'I pray you, do not fall in love with me,
For I am falser than vows made in wine'
(As You Like It – Act 3, Scene 5)

– WILLIAM SHAKESPEARE

Prologue

AN OLD MAN WITH TOO MUCH BOUNCE IN his step and sparkle in his eyes to ever be considered elderly, stood gazing out the window of his office on the second floor of his hotel. The Boutique Hotel Campo de' Fiori may have been a new name and one of the top hotels in Rome. But the heart and soul of the building, like that of the man, had not changed; it was as sound as it had been the day it had been built three centuries earlier.

The first ring came, and the gentleman jumped. He strutted over to his desk and lifted the handset of the telephone. After allowing the caller his fill of words, he said, "Yes, but we only have one room left." His gaze immediately shifted to an old photo on his desk: himself and three others, all four in their twenties, were handsomely dressed in anticipation of a party. After a short pause, he said, "I don't care who you are. I am Fabio Vitale, and this is my hotel now. What I say goes. If I say there is only one room left, then there is only one room left." He tried to suppress a laugh, but the soft genuine sound found its way into the receiver, over the ocean, and to the ears on the other side. The hotel owner's once pitch black hair had gone all white, but his laugh had not changed. Like every other part of him, it was filled with the bubbly intoxication of his lust for life. He waited for a response from the caller, and then said, "Goodbye," with a sly grin. After a pause, he added, "my old friend."

Chapter One

ON THE FLOOR NEXT TO AN OLD BROWN suitcase was a box. Michael Valentino brushed his hand across the eighteen years of dust, revealing the word *Trains*. Knowing his urge would probably make no sense to anyone else but him, he had to see them. He had only played with them for an hour on the Christmas morning he had received them, but it had been a magical hour. And that hour would repeat itself whenever he had had the chance to take out his trains. One day, he couldn't remember why or when, the trains had been boxed up and hidden away up in the attic ever since. Their house in Queens was too small to keep a model train setup year round. And after that first Christmas, he knew how his mother really hadn't wanted them out. He had gotten the trains from Santa, which meant both his parents. But since his father had been the one who had taken any interest at all in things that moved, Michael had always associated the trains with him. Michael lifted the tape from the box and opened it. He looked down on the old trains, then quickly smacked the cardboard lid and turned his face away.

The trains really meant nothing now that his father was dead. Michael hung on to an aching regret. It was stupid really, the argument that they had had and the months they hadn't spoken to one another afterwards. What he wouldn't do now for just a few words or a handshake. The whole argument was so stupid. It was about only six hundred dollars, and he had felt good giving the money to his father. But when his father gambled it away instead of paying his debt, Michael had lost what little respect he had left for him. And so the silence had begun. The visits to the house had become fewer and further between. Michael hated the fact that he wasn't seeing his mother, it wasn't her fault. She could forgive his father for his faults, in her strange way, but Michael couldn't. The lying that had bothered him the most. His father could be so convincing, and yet, so pathetic. Michael really hated that about him. He wanted an honest father, a father he could look up to. He stood and kicked something.

It was a smallish trunk made of dark brown weathered leather with two tan leather straps and brass buckles. Both straps were loosened from their buckles and the trunk's lid was askew. Michael was sure he had never seen the trunk before. A clear path in the dust ran across the top of it exposing a label inscribed with the word *Italy*. It was obvious that someone had opened the trunk recently, and the only one in his family who had ever been to Italy was his father. Michael paused to weigh his options, then kneeled and lifted the lid.

His father's old uniform was on top. Cleaned, pressed, and neatly folded, it was wrapped in a protective plastic. The brass buttons shone stunningly against the khaki material. Michael lifted the package. Under it was his father's army cap in a second plastic cover. He set those two on the floor and began digging through the rest of the trunk's contents. There wasn't really that much, just a few postcards, photos, and letters, and a newspaper printed on the day the war in Europe ended. The item that attracted his attention most was the cigar box. Recalling his father's fondness for enjoying cigars on the right occasion, Michael reached for the box. He used to cherish those times when his father would strike a match and puff on the end of his favorite cigar. It was always a moment when time had stopped. His father would slow down and enjoy the company of his son. He would talk with him and ask him questions about school and girls; he would pay attention to him. It had only happened once in a blue moon, so it was easy for Michael to remember.

He let the bottom of the cigar box rest in his left hand and brushed the fingers of his right one across the letters while mouthing the words on the label, *Luce della Luna*. He tested the box's weight by moving his hand up and down. It felt light. He lifted the cover and found a single dried-up cigar butt sitting on top of some of its loose leaves. He reached for it. It was brittle, so he brought it gently to his nose. The old familiar scent was faint, but still there. He smiled to himself and thought of some of the happy days with his father. There was no single day that had ever stood out in his mind as the best day with him. The happy days were all just fine.

With the cigar pressed up against his nose, Michael glanced down into the trunk. When he'd rustled its contents earlier, a black and white photograph had found its way on top of the other things. He bent over and peered down at the photo and then lifted it for examination. He saw an image of his father in his army clothes standing next to a young woman in a wide, knee-length dress. She had dark long hair and wore a very bright smile as she stared into the camera lens. Michael's father, also quite young at the time, was leaning over her with his hand on her very large belly. His eyes were on the lens as well, and his smile beamed wide. In the background. there was a nondescript café in what appeared to be a bustling location.

Michael turned the photo over to its back and read the caption. *Naples, May 1945 with Caterina. Who was Caterina?* He thought at first. But then more questions bounced around in his brain. Was his father dating this woman? Apparently. *Were they a couple? Or were they just friends? Was she pregnant?* Undoubtedly, from the clear bulge in her abdomen. His father wouldn't have had his hand on her stomach like that unless she were pregnant; it would be rude otherwise.

Michael peeked down into the trunk again and searched. He found another photo of what he was sure was his father with a young lady. He could not be sure if it were the same woman, because she and his father were kissing in the photo. He turned it over and it read *With Caterina at Sorrento, 1944.* Then a suspicion about the cigar box beat at his mind. He lifted the cigar box, turned it over, and dumped the dry leaves out. A faded card fell to the attic floor. He lifted the card and read *The first cigar from Caterina's father's shop in Naples. August, 1944.* It seemed to be adding up; Michael's father had had a love affair during the war with what was presumably a young Italian woman named Caterina. And she was very pregnant in the spring of 1945. *With dad's child?* he thought. It appeared that way. Caterina's father had owned a cigar shop in Naples where Michael's father bought his cigars. *Could that have been how they met? Did my father meet this sweet smiling Caterina, in her father's cigar shop?*

A third black and white photograph showed Michael's father and Caterina in front of a small shop sharing an ice cream cone. The ice cream was dribbling down her chin while Michael's father dabbed at it with his tongue. *Being silly with Caterina at Gay-Odin in Naples* it read on the back. And a fourth photo showed the couple raising their wine glasses in a toast while seated on metal chairs outside a café. *Toasting love at Caffe Gambrinus, Naples, 1944.*

Michael ruffled through the few postcards and letters. They were addressed to his grandparents who had lived in Brooklyn at the time of the Second World War. Michael pulled out one letter and read how he had met Caterina *seven months ago* at her father's shop while buying cigars, and how he had asked her to marry him. The words flowed beautifully as if his father was pouring out his heart to his parents. It seems he had an undying love for this young, smiling Italian girl. The letter was dated April 5th, 1945. Michael's father would marry Caterina and bring her back to New York with him. The evidence was overwhelming. Michael swept up the photos and letters, tucked them in his breast pocket, and raced to the attic stairs.

He hurried down the stairs to the dining room. His mother Rosa was there, arranging an overstuffed pot of cheese ravioli in the center of the table. "Mom," was all Michael could spit out before she dashed, one hand in the air, back into the kitchen. She quickly returned with a second huge pot filled to the brim with tomato sauce.

"Slide that pot holder over, would you?" she asked him, trying her best to nudge the thing a few inches to the left.

"Mom, I have to ask you something," said Michael, repositioning the pot holder.

"What is it?" said Rosa. Her eyes were on the table, fixed in the way they were always fixed when she was preparing dinner. She looked studious, like she was solving a puzzle.

"It's about Dad," said Michael. He took his seat on the side of the table opposite the entrance to the kitchen, to the right of his brother Louie.

She turned to face Michael and answered, "What about him, may he rest in peace?" She had taken on the addendum, adding it to every one of her references to her late husband. That was, when she didn't use, "may God have mercy on his soul." With both additions, she made the sign of the cross. She began dishing out the plates, which quickly circled the table.

I was looking at some of Dad's old things up in the attic," said Michael, "and I found something that's got me puzzled."

"What is it?" she asked, laying her eyes now on her first son. "Louie, you got enough raviolis?"

"Stop trying to make me fatter than I already am," said Louie, lightly slapping his stomach with both hands.

Michael uncorked a bottle of red wine and divvied it up into six glasses. He first offered the drink to his sisters Mia, Gabriella, and Jenny, and then to his brother. They each accepted a glass. He held up the sixth glass as an offering to his mother, but as usual, Rosa declined. Rosa never drank, not even Italian wine. He then offered a toast to everyone's health.

Mia helped dish out meatballs and tomato sauce, and then took a seat next to Jenny. But Rosa continued to stand, busying herself with fixing a salad and refreshing the antipasto platter. While the six family members were seated and had begun eating, Michael said, "Mom?" She didn't answer, so he looked his mother in the eye and asked, "Who's Caterina?"

Rosa dropped her fork. It clanged loud on the white porcelain plate. The others looked up and wondered what had happened. Rosa was always composed and always in charge. But the color flew from her cheeks and she was now shaking. Something was amiss. Then, tears welled up in her hazel eyes and she cleared her throat. She sniffed, and then said, "You know, your father wasn't always so quiet." She intentionally avoided Michael's question. "It wasn't until much later that he got that way. When he got sick. He was so much fun and so alive when we first got married. Everyone always said that the party didn't start until Little Joe got there. That's what everyone used to call him, 'Little Joe'. He was my Little Joe. Everyone loved him. I loved him." Rosa shook her head. "But that was a long time ago." She wiped her tears with the dish towel that was hanging over her left shoulder and said, "I don't know why it had to happen to him." She turned her far-off look back to Michael.

"I know," he said. "I'm sorry, Mom."

"Why did you have to say anything?" said Gabriella. "Look what you did. You upset mom." She started to stand, but Rosa stifled her daughter's worry with a push of air.

"It's all right," said Rosa, "It's all right." She breathed in long and deep and her eyes went to a faraway place.

"I haven't heard the name Caterina in…thirty years," said Rosa. "My God, has it been that long?" She chuckled softly to herself. "I thought it was gone and would never return."

"Who are you talking about, Mom?" asked Mia.

"Caterina," answered Rosa. "Your father's first love."

"What!" Rosa's children cried. Well, everyone cried, but Michael.

Rosa calmly nodded. "His first love," she said. "She was a woman he met in Italy during the war. How can I even say that? Woman," she scoffed. "Caterina was just a girl, only seventeen, I think, when they met." She looked down at the off-white, lace tablecloth and began drawing circles with her fingernails. Rosa snorted a short laugh and said, "Funny." She looked up at her five children.

"Funny?" asked Gabriella.

"They met," said Rosa, not really to any one of them, but more to herself. "He loved her. And she loved him."

"So what happened?" asked Mia.

"The war ended, and your father came home," answered Rosa. "And he never saw her again."

"That was it?" asked Louie. He turned to the right and faced Michael. "So what's the big deal?"

"I don't think 'that was it,'" answered Michael.

"What are you talking about?" said Louie.

Michael withdrew the contents of his breast pocket and let them fall to the table. He chose the photo of his father with his hand on the stomach of the very pregnant Caterina and held it up for the rest to see. "This," he said. "*This* is what I'm talking about. She was pregnant."

"Who was?" asked Jenny.

"Caterina," answered Michael, rotating the photo left and right. "And that's Dad with his hand on her belly."

"So?" said Louie.

Michael's glance shifted to his mother. "Mom?"

"Yes, she was pregnant with your father's child," said Rosa.

Mia threw her hand up to her mouth and gasped.

"Really?" said Gabriella.

"It's true," said Rosa. "She had your father's child, but he was already back in New York by then."

"So he didn't marry her," asked Michael, "like it says in the letter?"

"No," answered Rosa. "At least, that's what he told me. They were supposed to get married in the summer. But the war ended in May. And your father was among the first soldiers to come home."

"Why didn't he just marry her quick and bring her back to New York?" asked Jenny.

"I asked him that once," said Rosa. "All he said was, 'Never mind that now', and that was the end of that."

"But she did have his baby, right?" asked Mia.

"That's right."

All eyes were now on Rosa. "You have a half-brother," she said. "All of you. I don't even know his name. But I guess he'd be about thirty-two now."

"Wow, a half-brother," said Mia. "How about that? All the way over in Italy."

"Your father only spoke about him that one time, about a year after we were married, when I found the letter," said Rosa. "And never again. I think it was too painful for him."

"So Daddy never met him?" said Jenny.

"Never."

Louie shook his head, but said nothing.

"That's it. I'm going to Italy," said Michael, banging his hand on the table with the force of the idea.

"What!" cried Rosa. "Where did this plan come from?"

"I've just decided. I feel there's some unfinished business over there that Dad should have taken care of. I feel like I owe it to him, and to our half-brother."

Louie started to laugh. He bumped his glass, almost spilling the wine. "Are you nuts?" he said with a chuckle. "I think you had too much wine."

"I'm not drunk. And I'm not nuts," said Michael. "In fact, I've never been so sure of anything in my whole life. There's a reason I found that stuff up in the attic. Something made me go up there. Something made me look. I'm telling you—I'm meant to go to Italy to find my half-brother. Something out there's telling me I have to meet him. Something like...fate."

"Another one of your harebrained ideas," said Louie, shaking his head. He faced Rosa. "First he wanted to be a pilot, and then he wanted to join the Peace Corps." He glanced back at Michael. "But you've never been further than your own backyard."

"Go ahead and laugh all you want," said Michael. "I'm going to Italy this summer."

Rosa held her cheeks with both hands and moaned. *"Dio mio, you're crazy!"* she cried, and then shook her hand, fingertips touching, in the manner Italians do when they are frustrated. "Michael, you're going to bury me right next to your father," she said. She closed her eyes only for a short moment. "You can't go to Italy all by yourself. You don't know where you're going, and you can't even speak Italian. You're going to get yourself killed over there."

"Are you kidding?" said Jenny, with a wide grin. "I would love to go to Italy for a summer. I'm so jealous."

"You be quiet! You're not going anywhere," said Rosa, waving her index finger at Jenny. "And don't encourage him," she added. "He doesn't need any of that."

Then Mia shouted, "Please! Don't go! How can you think about leaving so soon after Daddy died?"

Louie mumbled, "Nothing more than pipe dreams."

"You've got something to say?" asked Michael.

"Nothing," said Louie. "I just don't want to see you make a mistake. Besides, you should be here now. Mom needs you."

"Mom's fine. She's got all of you," said Michael. He put his arm around Rosa's shoulder.

"And how do you know he's even in Italy?" asked Louie. "He could be anywhere. He could be here, for all you know. You'll never be able to find him, Mick."

"I don't care what you say. I'm going to Italy," said Michael.

"For Christ's sake, Mick!" bellowed Louie. He slammed his fork on the table and stared down his brother. "Our half-brother obviously doesn't want anything to do with us!"

"How do you know that?"

"Don't be stupid," said Louie. "Why would he want to know? If his mother told him about Dad, do you really think he'd want to meet us?"

"Maybe," said Michael. "How can I find out if I don't go?"

"There wouldn't happen to be any other reason why you're so bent on finding this half-brother, would there?" asked Louie.

"What do you mean?" asked Michael. He slowly sipped at his wine.

"You know."

"What are you saying?" said Michael.

"Do I have to spell it out for you?" said Louie.

"Yeah, spell it out for me, big brother," said Michael.

"Could it be possible that this quest you fantasize about to find our half-brother is really just a charade? Some big thing you think you're going to accomplish that really just exists so as to mask your pain?" asked Louie.

"You're crazy," said Michael. "You don't know what you're talking about. And you don't know about my pain."

"My God, Mick," said Louie. "You can't bring her back!"

"No, but maybe I can at least forget her," said Michael. "And I can find someone else who is lost to me." His heart was breaking all over again. His older brother had opened the wound that seemed to heal less, not more, with the passage of time.

"Does that really matter?" asked Louie. "When are you going to let it go, Mickey? When?"

"You're something, you know that? You think you got all the answers, huh, big brother?" said Michael. "But you don't. You don't know what it's like." He pointed a finger at Louie. "You just don't know." He took a deep, calming breath. "I'm going to Italy. And it's not because of my pain. It's because I want to find my half-brother." But Michael wouldn't allow the truth to escape. He didn't want Louie to have the satisfaction of knowing he was right.

"Waste of time," said Louie. "And money." He chuckled dryly, swiping at the remnants of tomato sauce on his plate with a slice of bread.

"That's okay. It's my time. And my money," replied Michael. "You don't have to believe. All that matters is that I do."

Louie sat shaking his head, crunching on his salad now. "It's been more than thirty years," he said. "He's all grown up. You don't even know what he looks like. And you've never even been to Italy. You don't know the language. You don't know the culture. You're out of your mind. It'll be like trying to find a tiny clown fish in the ocean, and you don't even know how to swim."

"Your brother's right, Michael," said Rosa. "You don't know anything about Italy. It might be dangerous. And I don't want to see you get disappointed."

Michael tilted his head back and drained his wine glass. "I'll find him," he said. "I will." He reached for the dark green bottle of wine, poured himself another glass, and before indulging said, "I'll find him. I'm a good swimmer."

Chapter Two

EVERY MAP, GUIDE BOOK, AND PHOTO Michael had studied over the past five months was imprinted in his mind. He could think of nothing else. He twisted and turned, unable to find comfort in the airplane seat. But the sound of a piercing laugh nearby didn't help his mood. It started out as a light-hearted giggle, coming from the other side of the cabin and four seats ahead. He craned his neck, trying to blink the figure clear. But all he could see was the back of a woman's head, with long straight hair. He surmised she was getting a laugh from the in-flight movie. Michael tried to ignore it, and her, but the incessant giggling transformed into a high-pitched squeaky cackle and unnerved him. It was the only sound other than the hum of the jet's engines, and it was impossible to escape.

The silhouetted head was indeed that of an adult woman. He forced his gaze out the window and willed the irritation away. He would soon be off this plane since it was only flying from Rome to Naples. Michael knew that the memory of the annoying sound would vanish like a light dusting of snow on an early spring day.

He looked out the window. He could see nothing but clouds beneath the plane and his thoughts turned to the argument he had had months earlier with his brother Louie. *Why couldn't I just admit it?* he thought. *I could be so damned stubborn sometimes. Louie was right. It's going to be impossible to find my brother. What in the world was I thinking?* As the clouds rushed by, Michael told himself that he would ease the aching hole in his chest and find joy in Italy instead.

The wheels touched down with a screech, and then the gleaming green and white jet was safely on the ground. Twisting right and left at the waist, Michael slowly blinked the grogginess from his eyes (he hadn't slept a wink on the flight from New York to Rome), stretched his neck, then shoulders and back. The plane came to a stop at its designated gate. He unbuckled his seat belt and stood, cracking the joints in his ankles and knees. A halted parade of passengers bottlenecked in both aisles.

And then the laugh passed him. He cringed. He thought he had heard the last of it. But there it was, unmistakable, the same grating sound that had bothered him during the flight. Only now he could clearly see that the grating laugh had belonged to the woman with the long black hair. As the tall lean woman stood in the aisle, her torso swirled, and her limbs reached up for her bag. Michael drank in her milky white complexion and perfectly straight nose. She was slender and shapely, like a department store mannequin. *It ought to be illegal for anyone to look that good*, he thought.

The mannequin girl smiled slightly at the passengers waiting behind her and set her bag down on her seat. Michael reached up for his own bag, shaking his head on the way down. He thought to himself how perfect people like the mannequin woman always had something wrong with them. They were always full of themselves and stuck-up, or something even worse. He was sure that there was something about those perfectly beautiful people that made them ugly deep down inside. Mannequin Woman grasped her manicured fingers around the handle of her bag, adjusted the silk scarf around her neck, and inched her way down the narrow aisle. He was glad she wasn't going to be around long enough for him to find out what it was that made her so ugly. And Michael put her, and her maddening laugh, out of his mind.

Chapter Three

OWNED AND OPERATED BY THE SAME FAM-
ily since 1870, L'Antica Pizzeria da Michele featured only two
types of pizza, the marinara and the margherita. Nothing else.
With a nod from an apron-clad pizza-maker, Michael seated
himself at one of the white marble tables with a black metal
frame. The green and white tile walls were covered in photos of
famous celebrities and ran up to the unadorned white ceiling.
Michael scanned the dining space and noticed a cook repairing
a loose hinge on the kitchen door with a brown bag. Nimble
waiters with steamy pies in hand glided smoothly across the
white ceramic floor. The smoking-hot rounds sailed out of
the smoldering wood-burning oven every two minutes or less.
They were each twelve inches around with thin charred crusts
that were both fluffy and chewy. The mozzarella cheese on
Michael's margherita was clean and fresh as a daisy in spring,
as if there had been a dairy farmer at work behind the pizzeria

somewhere. A speedy waiter dropped off a bottle of beer and Michael began pouring the golden drink into his glass. Then he brought the glass to his lips.

"Are you sure you want to do that?" asked a tall woman behind him. As he turned, she laid her hand over his and eased the glass back down to the table. "The Italians here in Naples are all crazy. They can't be trusted around your drink."

He eyed her suspiciously and said, "It's just beer."

"Who knows what they put in their beer?" she said.

"It's bottled." He shrugged.

"I wouldn't drink it."

"I'm not you."

She sighed, loud enough for him to take notice.

"I'm sorry," he said. He stood and scanned the room. "Are you here alone?"

"I am."

"In that case," he said, "would you care to join me?" He gestured at the chair opposite his. "You know, for a beer."

She snorted softly. "I'd love to."

Michael pulled the chair out for her. "I'm Michael," he said as she carefully took her seat. She was tall, but not over-ly tall, one or two inches shorter than him. Her hair was long, straight, and very dark brown. The manicured ends fell to her lower back. Her skin was pure white, without a blemish or a freckle to be found. With her manicured fin-gers, she laid her small black purse on the end of the small white table.

"Camille," she said. "I was named after a character in an old stage play. It was popular in Paris in the late nineteenth century. My mother enjoys the arts."

"So you're French?" Michael eased her chair in so she was closer to the table and scooted around to the opposite side. He sat and looked her in the eyes.

"By default," she said. "Though, I always wished I could have been born in Paris."

Michael looked up at the passing waiter and raised his glass. He tapped it with the other hand and the waiter brought a second glass. Michael poured the pale liquid into her glass now. "Now, if what you say is true about people in Naples, this may be my last meal. And yours. What do you say we at least go out enjoying it?" He tapped his glass into hers and drank a large mouthful of the bubbling bitterness.

"All right. But I sure hope you know what you're doing." Camille took a small sip.

He feigned a cough and under his breath said, "Me, too."

They looked at each other and shrugged. Michael gestured to his pizza pie and they each reached for a slice. They smacked them together like champagne flutes and bit into them. At first, they didn't speak a word to each other. There were only short indistinct mumbles and punctuated savory groans colliding in the hot dense air. They became swept away by the intoxicating allure of this uncomplicated food. After he finished his first slice, Michael stood up, looked around and proclaimed, "This is truly the world's greatest pizza!"

"How do you know?" she asked laughing. "Have you had pizza all over the world?"

The other patrons did not seem to be bothered by Michael's passionate display. They merely glanced up at him, nodded in agreement, and continued stuffing their faces with pieces of their own steamy pies.

"No. And now I don't have to travel the world," answered Michael. "I've already found the very best slice." He took his seat with a regal air and they clinked glasses a second time.

"So, you're not from France originally," he said, taking up a second slice.

"I was born in the U.S.," she said, "in the south. Of the New Orleans Beauchamps, a name of some prominence, you could say."

"Ah," said Michael. He felt that if he didn't already know what he was up against with Camille, now he had no doubt.

"You?"

"I'm a die-hard New Yorker, I guess you'd say," he answered.

Camille positioned a second slice on the aluminum tray, but did not raise it from the table. Finishing her glass of beer, she said, "I live there now, on the east side."

"How about that?" said Michael. "My place is on the west side."

"I guess we're like the wicked witches over there," said Camille. She tapped on her empty glass and he filled it. Then he filled his, and signaled to the waiter to bring two more bottles.

They emptied their glasses with a single pull just in time for the other two bottles to arrive. Camille grinned while Michael poured. He chewed on his second slice of pizza a bit more, but focused mainly on the beer. Camille let her slice lay still, and seemed fine with allowing it to get cold. The heat was really too much; she was out to quench her parched throat.

After finishing off a second bottle and beginning on a third, Camille and Michael were feeling pretty good. The heat would linger outside and the beer would stay cold inside. Impatient, Camille tried pouring into her glass now, but missed completely. The golden ale spilled, fizzing up on the white table. The waiter happened by and dabbed at it with a towel. He was off to another table soon enough, leaving the two foreigners to themselves.

Michael grabbed at the opportunity. "So what brings you to Naples? You know, where all the crazy people are."

"Just slumming around."

He looked her over, head to foot. And those feet were adorned in shiny, black high heels. A red skirt fell just below the knees, and a white silk blouse clung lovingly to her moist torso. Around her neck was a dainty, silk scarf with a pastel floral design. "No," he said, "Not with that getup. In fact, I bet you've never been slumming in your life, have you?"

"All right,'" she answered, "I've got one week…hmm, what would you call it?" She looked at her polished fingers on the wet glass, then back at him. "A week of freedom."

He jerked his head to one side, looking puzzled.

"One week, in which I get to do all the things I want to do," she said. "Maybe even some I never knew I wanted to do."

"Sounds like fun," he said. "And then?"

"Then I get married, of course," she said.

"Why of course?"

"Isn't that what you're supposed to do? When you're in love?"

"I guess," he said. "But it wasn't exactly like that with me. Not the soul-possessing kind of love some people talk of."

"Ah. Too bad," she said.

"I suppose it is," said Michael. "You're heading back to New York then, after the week of freedom?"

She shook her head. "No. To Paris. That's where Claude is. He's the French one."

"Ah. Gotcha."

"And you?"

"Me?"

"What are you doing here, in Naples?"

"Oh." Michael rubbed his right shoulder with his left hand. "I'm looking for someone."

"A wife?"

"Not exactly," he said. "It's my half-brother."

"Oh."

"Yeah, I didn't even know I had one until a few months ago," he said. "Now I'm here searching."

"It looks like we've got our week planned out then."

"Looks like it."

She pressed her hand over his and looked into his eyes with pursed lips. "You didn't really think this love affair of ours could last more than a brief encounter, did you, my darling?" she joked.

He snorted a short chuckle. Then Michael leaned over the table, filled his hands with her jaws, and gently brought her face towards his. Her pouty lips plumped up further. He pursed his lips, but then drew back. "A stallion must run free," he said. He pulled his hands away.

Camille threw her arm up and rested the back of her wrist on her forehead. "Whatever am I to do without you, my darling?" she said.

Michael could hold back the laughter no longer. And not a moment after he chuckled, Camille let go of a long squeaky cackle.

It couldn't be, he thought.

Scrutinizing her, his *couldn't be* fast turned into *has to be*. The long dark hair was the same. The straight nose was the same. The alabaster skin, the lean shapely figure and the silk scarf around the neck. How could he have missed it? Mannequin Woman from the plane had somehow found him here at this pizzeria.

He decided it didn't matter, since all he knew about her was her first name and the fact that she was going to be married in Paris in one week. He'd quickly ditch her, once the beer was gone. *So better to drink up and bid her farewell.*

Michael cleared his throat. He stood. He slipped the black leather jacket that had been resting on the back of his chair over his shoulders and a wedge formed in Camille's brow. "What's with the jacket? It's a hundred degrees out there."

"It's symbolic," he said. "I wear it for someone else. It's silly really." He stuffed his hands in the pockets, and a memory from just a few months earlier rushed back to him.

His mother had suggested that the two of them go up to the attic and share what they could of what was left of his father's memory and he jumped at the chance. However, he was more than a bit surprised that his mother wanted to revisit his father's past life in Italy before she'd met him. And so, they ran their eyes over the rest of the photographs taken in Italy and scanned his father's old letters that he sent to his parents back home. It was then that they stumbled across the black, leather jacket Michael's father had worn as a young man. It was worn and faded, but it was still a perfectly functional jacket. Michael had asked his mother about it, and she explained that his father had only worn it in Italy, whenever he had had a date with Caterina. His father was so tired of wearing his uniform day and night, and whenever he had leave, he wore the leather jacket. It was a favorite of Caterina's, and Michael's father never wore it back home in New York.

"Symbolic," said Camille. "Or, you know, whatever you say."

Michael nodded. As she stood, he scooted around behind her and slid her chair out so she could stand. "Well, I guess this is goodbye," he said. "I've got to find my half-brother, and you've got your wedding, so."

"So." Her perfectly tweezed eyebrows hitched up and she shrugged her perfectly formed shoulders.

"Shouldn't we pay for the pizza?" she asked.

"I got it." He pulled out his wallet and left more than enough cash on the table.

Once outside, instead of parting ways, they tottered along together for a few minutes since they'd decided they would head back to the hotel. (They were both, incidentally, staying at the same hotel that was called the Excelsior down at the southern tip of the city. It was on the gulf near that castle that had something to do with an egg.) When Michael moved ahead, he noticed that Camille looked like some high wire circus performer on her heels. He turned to see the tipsy girl bent over, and fiddling with one of her black shoes. He shook his head, turned back and continued on, ignoring the day's colorful laundry flying from the balconies of the old brick and concrete homes. With Camille still trailing behind, they made their way down three narrow, tree-lined blocks and then, they came to a fork in the road. Peering down each path, Michael finally said, "It's this way," pointing to the right, but he was directing them with nothing more than a hunch.

"What is?" she called ahead.

"We'll see."

That path led to a cobblestone street and many more trees. They were lemon trees, to be exact. And the shimmering sky held a full moon in place. It was faint and translucent, but very large. And it was hanging low in the afternoon sky. But neither Michael nor Camille spotted it. Meanwhile, a lagging Camille attempted to negotiate the countless cracks in the cobblestones with her shiny black heels. He turned back a few times to encourage her to speed up, but his badgering only made things worse. While she was looking at him she got her right heel caught in the stones. And she called up ahead and blamed him.

"What do you want me to do about it? It's your shoe," he yelled back, and kept right on walking.

"You're not going to help me?" she asked, staring down the path in amazement.

He stopped, turned back, and with irritation written all over his face, answered, "Just yank your foot out."

"I'm not going to yank my foot. A lady doesn't *yank*." She crossed her long lean arms in front of her heaving chest.

"Just do it!" he barked back.

Frustrated and embarrassed by the fact that he was unwilling to help, Camille gritted her teeth and wrenched her foot from the crack in the cobblestones, so vigorously that her shoe flew from her foot, soared up into the air, and wedged itself in the spiny branches of one of the lemon trees. With her right leg dangling in mid air, she glared down the stony road at him.

"Don't expect me to go up there," chuckled Michael, jabbing a thumb into his chest. "I was never any good at climbing trees. I'm a city boy," he finished, his breathing labored from the beer.

Camille released her anger and with her eyes half closed, said, "Well, *I* can't go. I only have one shoe." Clutching her leg under the thigh, she laughed at her predicament. This sort of thing would have normally had her in an outrage, but for some reason, now it was strangely amusing. She wondered if she was relaxed by the beer, or perhaps because of him, and his stubborn and careless attitude. She found herself actually drawn to the notion that he did not come to her rescue right away. Her white knight, Claude, would have been up that tree before she could have said *lemon*. But Michael's callousness, which should have irked her, put a surprising smile on her face and landed a thumping weightlessness on her heart.

"Hell of an argument you've got there, lady," he said, backtracking. Grumbling to himself, he removed his jacket and shirt and held them at arm's length, leaving his chest covered only by a thin, white, tank-top undershirt. "Here, hold these," he said.

She set her leg down and rested her naked foot on the covered toes of her other foot while she grabbed his jacket and shirt.

He started to climb, but he slid right back down the tree, his inner thighs skidding along the bumpy trunk. Camille let out a long, squeaky cackle. In spite of himself and that abrasive annoyance, he enjoyed a hearty laugh as well. "I'm probably going to be sore tomorrow. And that'll be your fault too." Now glaring at her, he rubbed his thighs, then inched his way up a second time. Camille was unable to keep herself from examining his bunching arms and shoulders, his muscles rippled and contracted as he grabbed branch after branch. She exhaled nervously and swiped at the perspiration around the scarf around her neck. In his intoxicated state, he climbed on, knocking a cluster of the lemons loose that came barreling down on poor Camille.

"Hey, watch it!" she yelled up the tree.

He stopped climbing for a moment to look down. "Sorry!" he yelled back, not meaning it one bit. When Camille caught his sly smirk, she bent over, lifted three lemons off the ground, and flung them, one at a time, into his tree. But her aim was about as accurate as her laugh was charming. Michael swatted away the lemons that came nearest him easily enough. She shook an angry fist at him and he grinned broader.

Michael resumed his climb until he reached the branch with the black shoe. He rested an elbow on the leafy branch and it dipped down. His fingers inched along and he tested the tree's grip on the shoe. "Are you kidding me?" he grumbled. Then he turned down to her, he complained, "You had to have spiky heels, didn't you? The damn thing is stuck!" He jerked powerfully at the shoe's curvy sole, but the determined tree branch would not relinquish its hold.

"So pull on it!" she called up with a chortle.

"You pull on it!" he roared, realizing immediately after that the remark had made no sense. But he was drunk, and didn't care. "It's wedged in! It's stuck, woman!"

"Okay! I'm coming up." Camille removed her other shoe, allowed the jacket and shirt to drop near it. Then she bunched her skirt up around her hips, and hugged the tree at its base. Laughing hysterically at herself, she instantly slid back down the few measly inches she had climbed.

Her screech soared up the tree to his waiting ears. "You're crazy!" He shouted back down to her. "You can't climb a tree in a skirt, you ninny!"

"I could to," she replied. "Only if you weren't so drunk." She let go of the bristly trunk and fell to the ground, landing on her backside, and then tumbling onto her back. Her red skirt flew up above her waist and over her face. Michael could not resist a peek, and immediately guffawed at prissy Miss Perfect from the south on her derrière in the middle of this charming Italian town with her frilly pink panties on display.

"You mean if *I* weren't so drunk," he called down to her, now hanging precariously from the bending branch.

Camille grappled with the cumbersome skirt, slowly righting herself on the small patch of grass. Smoothing down frizzy black strands of her hair, she yelled up, "That's what I said. If you weren't so drunk."

After cackling his fill, Michael turned back to the job at hand. He steadied himself on the swaying branch, and finally wrenched the spiky shoe free. "Just sit tight. I got it!" he cried.

An elderly couple nearing the tree stopped. The short, chunky grandmother peered up at Michael, and her taller, jovial husband gazed down at the long-haired beauty flat on her bottom with a pile of lemons haphazardly surrounding her. He asked in English if she needed any help, and she replied, "Oh, it's just a game we like to play." Then she lifted a lemon and pretended to throw it up at Michael. Shaking their heads at the foolish foreigners, the old couple silently continued on their way.

Michael gripped the shoe in his right hand, pausing to consider how he was going to get down using only one hand. Instead, he drew the shoe to his mouth and bit down hard on the shiny leather, and shimmied down the tree. He landed next to Camille on the small patch of grass. He was sopping wet with the perspiration. It'd soaked well down into his trousers, staining them a dark khaki. "Here you go, Cinderella. I'm betting it's a perfect fit."

"I don't know anymore, with your ugly teeth marks in it," she said.

"Ah, don't be such a baby. I got it for you, didn't I?" He slipped it on her right foot and silently gazed on her alabaster features, considering just how Cinderella-like she seemed at that precise moment. Barefoot and slumped on her backside, her red skirt soiled with a hearty green grass stain from a Naples side street. "You're some Cinderella. It seems she has lost both shoes."

"I didn't lose it," she said, "I took the other one off so I could climb the dumb tree."

"And what a mighty fine job you did."

"Are you always this sarcastic?" asked Camille.

"I get sarcastic when I'm drunk." But he was only acting this way because he was becoming more and more engrossed in the young firebrand who, to his ever-increasing aversion, had already been spoken for.

"Then you must be drunk all the time," said Camille, her eye for an eye tactic all she really had at her immediate disposal.

"Oh, good one!" said Michael. He stood and offered his hand in peace. Camille took hold of his hand and stared into his eyes, but quickly glanced away. It was too much. There was something about the way he looked at her that was very real. It was almost as if she had known those deep brown eyes before like he was a friend from a long time ago. She shook the peculiar thought from her mind, hopped over to her left shoe and slowly eased her foot in.

She twisted on the balls of her feet and checked her footing by digging both heels in the dirt. Then she smoothed out her soiled skirt and looked around in a most dignified manner. "Where were we going anyway?" she asked.

"I'm looking for my half-brother," he answered. "I don't know about you."

He bent over to retrieve his shirt and jacket. He slid his arms through the shirt's sleeves and tied the jacket around his clammy waist. "I saw the street before I went into the pizzeria. I think it's this way." He offered his hand and said, "Come on."

Camille braced herself as she pressed her hand into his. But then she immediately jerked her hand away and lifted it up to her ear, pretending to scratch an itch. "I'm all right," she said, miffed with herself over the sudden, inexplicable emotions. "Let's just go."

Chapter Four

THE NEXT MORNING, MICHAEL ENJOYED A relaxing breakfast at the hotel. Cappuccinos made to order were brought to his table, while he had selected a croissant and an apricot tart to accompany his two fried eggs, ham, cheese, and sliced fruit. The beer from the night before hadn't given him a hangover, but he felt tremendously hungry for some reason. He assumed it must have been from the eleven hours of sleep he'd indulged in after collapsing on his bed. The night had been an extremely warm one, but he had slept through it without event. After he had his fill at breakfast, he said goodbye to the stout grandmother who had served him and bounced out the front door of the hotel.

He started down the wide boulevard on the left. He'd decided that his walk would take him about twenty minutes (assuming the directions he had received from Alessandro, the front desk clerk with the wandering eyes, were correct).

He didn't mind the extra time. It would allow him to clear his head and fix in his mind a plan on how to approach the owner of the cigar shop, whoever that might be. About fifteen minutes into the walk, he noticed the clean, wide streets had turned into much narrower ones that were not exactly disgusting, but not that picturesque either. Laundry hung above his head and out the windows of third and fourth floor apartment buildings, vendors were hawking their various wares (there was a store for just about anything you could name or imagine), and small grocery and sweets shops spilled samples into the hands of the many pedestrians.

Michael squeezed his way around them and turned a half-right onto an angular street. About three quarters of the way down the narrow alley, he spotted the single-story building he had seen in his father's photograph. Spewing at tan stones at its base were dazzling blue-violet irises, and a small wooden sign that read SOUVENIR DI LUIGI jutted out from the old wall. *Luigi's Souvenirs?* Michael thought. Did he have the wrong address? He looked around and confirmed in his mind that he couldn't have. This was indeed the correct street and the correct building. But where were the words LUCE DELLA LUNA, the brand name of the old cigars?

He scanned the exterior quickly before entering the small shop. This had to be the place. Inside, a man in his early fifties with broad shoulders and a grey-white beard stood behind a wood counter guarding tattered, old humidors housing fine, expensive cigars. *Cigars! I was right.* But as his

eyes darted around the shop, he could see that the few cigars behind the counter were the only ones in the store. The
racks and shelves held postcards, knickknacks, tee-shirts, refrigerator magnets, and cute espresso pots in bright colors.
It really was a souvenir shop.

"*Avete bisogno d'aiuto?*" asked the bearded man.

Michael knew he'd have to speak Italian now, which only
made him more self-conscious. He had studied the language
and the Italian customs, but how much can one learn in a
few months? He hesitated to speak. But if he said nothing,
he would learn nothing. "*Sto cercando per il proprietario,*" he
said, in New York-accented Italian. He worried how the man
would react.

But the man stared without a word.

Michael pointed to himself. "Oh, is it my accent?" he
asked.

The bearded man held up his hands and shrugged.

Then Michael repeated, "*Sto cercando il proprietario.* The
owner. I'm looking for the owner, Signor Bagliore."

"Ah!" A huge smile lit up his manly face as the bearded
man spread his arms in an animated gesture. "Bagliore. Si, si!
Luigi Bagliore." With a grin from ear to ear, he thumped on
his chest three times with a heavy fist.

"Ah! Signor Bagliore! *Come sta? Mi chiamo* Michael
Valentino, from New York."

"*Bravo!*"

"You speak English, yes?"

"Yes, English, little." Signor Bagliore indicated with a small space between his thumb and index finger. "Welcome my shop." He brought his left hand to his breast like he was pledging his undying devotion to his one true love.

"Great! Wonderful! Thank you," said Michael. "I'm so happy to be here." He shook the man's hand, and without a second to think, dug his hand into his pants pocket and pulled a very old and faded cigar wrapper from his brown wallet. The brand was called *Luce della Luna*, which meant "moonlight," and it was the only cigar his father ever smoked. "Signor Bagliore, do you make these cigars?"

Michael gently placed the faded wrapper in the shop owner's hand, and the man studied the worn drawing of a full moon. His nod had Michael smiling. Though the label was old and worn, the gentleman had recognized it for certain. "*Si.* Yes, I know this cigar," he answered.

Giddy over his good fortune, Michael asked with a large grin, "Can I buy? I want to buy, two boxes." He held up two fingers.

The bearded man now looked puzzled. He stroked his beard, turned back as if he was checking his stock of cigars behind him, but then faced Michael again. "I cannot."

"Why not?"

"I do not have."

"What do you mean?"

"Owner took with him."

"The *owner?*"

Signor Bagliore nodded.

"Wait. I don't understand," said Michael, "I thought *you* were the owner."

"*Si,*" he said, and held up two fingers. "Second owner. First owner left."

"Left? What do you mean left?"

"He move away," said the bearded man. "He sell me the shop, and he move away."

Michael pointed at the man's chest. "But your name is Bagliore."

"*Si,* same name," replied the man.

"He's a different man, then."

"*Si,* different man, same name."

"Your father? Your brother?"

"No." Signor Bagliore waved his hand. "No father, no brother. Different man, same name.

"Whoa." Michael scratched the side of his head. "I didn't anticipate that," he said, more to himself than anyone else. Then he turned back to face Signor Bagliore. "So where did the first owner move?" he asked.

"Roma," answered the man.

"Rome?"

"*Si. Roma,*" said Bagliore. "First owner born there, and his family there for many years. In Via dei Cappellari."

"I guess I'm off to Rome then," said Michael.

"That's it?" asked Bagliore. "You just go?"

"Well…Why not?" said Michael. "It's why I came to Italy in the first place, to find my half-brother. If the first owner knows about my half-brother, then I have to find him."

"If you going, why not you check out Hotel Campo de' Fiori?"

"Why?"

"You will need a place to stay, no?" asked Bagliore.

"Well, sure, I guess," said Michael.

The shop owner smirked. He said, "Then stay there. It is really nice place."

"All right," said Michael. "Where is it?"

"Near Campo de' Fiori."

"Well, yeah, but where's that? Do you have the address?"

"Many flowers there," said the owner. "You can't miss it. You see when you arrive."

"I guess I will."

"*Si*. Then go to the house of first owner."

"I know. Same name, different man," said Michael.

" *Si*. Bring flowers to him," said the bearded Bagliore. "I remember, he like flowers."

"Do you have *his* address?"

"I forget."

"Of course you do."

"You want I should forget more?"

"No, no, I'm sorry," said Michael. "I shouldn't have said that. You've done a lot for me. I thank you. Really."

"*Prego*," replied Bagliore, adding a proud but sincere smile. "You ask for owner's address at the hotel."

"I guess I'm off then," said Michael, turning to view the front door of the shop.

When Michael turned back, Signor Bagliore said, "You no forget, bring flowers."

Michael shook the man's hand and replied, "I won't forget. Goodbye. And thank you again." And he was out the door of the shop on his way back to the Hotel Excelsior. He knew he'd have a quiet night to prepare for his journey to Rome in the morning.

Chapter Five

QUIET WAS ACTUALLY THE OPPOSITE KIND of a night Michael had. He wasn't through the entrance to the hotel and five steps into the lobby when he ran into Camille. Actually, it was more like he'd picked up on her sound rather than ran into her. He'd heard that unending cackle and it'd immediately alerted him to her. When she spotted him, she squealed for a good two seconds and shouted, "My goodness! Isn't this a hoot!"

"A hoot?"

"Sure," she replied, sauntering to greet him as he made his way up the steps. She was balancing a half-filled martini glass in her right hand. "Who would have thought we'd see each other again, my darling?"

He sighed. "What are the odds?"

"You are funny," she said, wrapping her arm around his waist. "But you already know that, don't you?" She checked his eyes.

"Yes, ma'am."

"Ma'am? What century are *you* living in, honey? We're in the seventies, and we females have been liberated." She raised her glass so it was even with the top of her head.

"I'll drink to that," said Michael, as the two of them made their way toward the small bar. It was dimly lit with an additional few candles and there was a tiny Italian man was softly tinkering at the piano. Two other couples were each separately enjoying the romantic quiet. Michael led Camille to a leather-padded bar stool and they sat. He ordered a Kamikaze in a Collins glass and removed his leather jacket.

"Wasn't that supposed to be symbolic?" said Camille pointing to the jacket.

He slipped it under his buttocks and said, "Right. But it's too darn hot for it now."

Camille cleared her throat and looked down at her glass. "This is nearly empty, my darling," she said, "isn't there anything you'd like to do about that?"

Michael gestured to the bartender who was eyeing them in the mirror that was fixed on the wall behind the bar. The bartender caught Michael's signal and nodded.

The drinks arrived, and, taking up her martini, she said, "You know, you never told me your name. But even when you do tell me, you'll always be my darling."

"It's Michael," he answered, raising his glass.

"I never would have guessed. I had you pegged for a Tony, or a Vinny, you know? One of those real New York Italian names." She eyed his features. "You're Italian, right?" She clanged her glass into his.

"How'd you know?"

They both swallowed some of their liquid.

"You're in Naples searching for your half-brother. It doesn't take a private eye to put it together."

"Yeah, but I won't be in Naples too much longer."

"Uh-oh. No luck finding him?"

"None."

"I guess you'll be heading home then?"

"Not yet," he said, and then he took another sip. He set his drink down on the bar and watched the sweaty beads run down the outside of the glass. "I got a tip today that's going to take me to Rome."

"Rome?" she cried.

The bartender glared at her and she threw her fingers up to hide her lips. "Sorry," she said and began giggling a tiny giggle.

No. Don't laugh, don't laugh, Michael thought. *I can't handle it.*

Turning to Michael, she whispered, "That's fantastic!"

"It is?"

"Of course, my darling," she said. "Maybe we'll happen upon each other there too."

"What do you mean?"

"I've booked myself the 9:50 train to Rome tomorrow morning. Didn't I tell you I was going?"

"It must have slipped your mind," he said, "with all that shoe-shopping you had to do."

"I knew you didn't forget about that." Camille grinned, twisted herself free from the bar, and sat with her feet extended to display a pair of shiny, new, red sandals with pointed heels. "Do you like them, my pet? I just knew you would."

"I'm your pet now?"

"You're anything I want you to be," she said, swiveling herself back to face the bar.

"I see how this is going to go."

"Good," she said, banging her glass into his again. "This is my week of freedom. Therefore, I make my own rules."

They drank and Michael said, "That's exactly why I'll be on an earlier train to Rome."

"Suit yourself, my sweet," she replied, "but we shall most definitely encounter each other again."

"You're sure about that?" A half-smile began to creep into the left side of his face.

"Of course. It's only Rome. How big can it be? Surely it's not another New York."

"I don't know," he said, with a shrug, "I'll find out when I get there."

"And so shall I." She downed the remains of her drink. "Well, good night, my darling," she said, swaying herself on the stool. "Or should I say *buona notte*, as they say here?"

He slid his hands under her armpits and eased her down to the grey marble floor. He peeked down at her feet in her shiny red shoes. And then he stole a glance at her calves. They were a brilliant white, whiter even than her smooth shoulders. "*Buona notte, mia cara*," he said.

"*Cara*?" she said, stepping back and away while smoothing down her dress.

"It means 'dear' or 'darling'," he answered.

"Now, I'll have to remember that," she said, shaking her head. "My Italian is so poor."

"Oh, I don't think there's anything poor about you," he said, shaking his head.

"We'll just have to see, won't we?" she said, and then she swayed her perfectly contoured hips in her perfectly shapely red dress as she walked away toward the elevator.

I've got to ask the front desk for an early wakeup call, he thought. *I can't be on her train if I'm going to function.*

Chapter Six

EARLY THE NEXT MORNING, THE ELEVATOR doors swished open on the lobby floor and Michael pranced out. He was pleased thinking he was about to be stretched out and relaxed on a First Class train to Rome. That was more his style than those cramped coach seats on the plane. With his single bag hanging from his shoulder, he made his way up to the front desk whistling a happy tune.

"*Buongiorno*," said the clerk. She was a young lady, more cute than pretty with a set of wavy dark bangs.

"*Buongiorno*," replied Michael.

"Are you checking out, *signore*?" she asked.

"Yes, I called down last evening to make the arrangements. Valentino?"

"Yes, I have it here." She rustled the papers in front of her on the desk.

"Good." Michael sent her a soft smile. "And my train reservation?"

"*Signore*—," began the woman, but she was interrupted by another hotel guest who had just emerged from behind a green marble pillar.

"Darling!" cried Camille.

"My goodness," muttered Michael, "not again."

"Yes, me again, darling," she said. "I can hear your every word, you know."

"How lucky for me."

"You are in luck, my sweet. It is a glorious day. The sun is shining. The birds are singing. And we are on our way to Rome!"

"On separate trains? You do recall that part, right, my pet?"

"Darling, you have not heard?"

"Heard what?" asked Michael.

Camille turned her attention to the front desk girl. "Carlotta, did you not tell the *signore* about the trains?"

"I tried to, but —," started the girl.

"Yes, I know, my darling," she said to Carlotta. "I will inform him."

"*Grazie.*"

"It seems that the train people have decided to take a *siesta*, as they say."

"*Siesta?*" Michael asked.

"A strike, my beloved," said Camille. "You do know what a strike is."

"Yes, the trains are on strike. Again," said the clerk.

Michael sighed out his frustration and then slipped his bag from his shoulder and set it down on the floor. "That's just great."

"But it *is* great," said Camille. "For we now get to travel to Rome via an alternate way."

"And just what might that be?"

"Vehicular transport, my darling."

"What?"

"Automobile, my pet, automobile."

"You mean rent a car?"

"Now you're catching on."

Carlotta instantaneously sprung into action. In her most assured voice, she said, "I can make a car rental reservation for you, *signore*, if you so desire."

Michael's eyes widened. Remaining composed, he replied, "Yes, I desire."

"*Bene.*" The clerk telephoned the rental service and spoke only a few words in Italian. She muffled the handset against her chest and said, "I am sorry, signore, but there is one car only. *Mi dispiace.*"

"What do you mean 'one car'?" asked Michael.

The clerk smiled apologetically and said, "The *signore* at the car rental, he say there are no more cars today. He have only one. It is summer season now. I hope she is okay." She stopped abruptly, allowing those words as her only explanation.

"Well, in that case, I think we shall take it," said Camille, forcing on the attendant a confident, cocky smirk.

"*We?*" blasted Michael. "What's all this *we* business? I fly, or in this case, drive, solo."

"Not today, darling," said Camille. She brushed his cheek with a tender finger. "You see, I don't drive."

"What?!"

"Driving is for… well, it's a skill that eludes me."

"What you're saying is it's beneath you."

"You're quite clever, my pet," said Camille, while gesturing to the bell man by waving her finger. "I knew there was a reason why I keep you close."

The bellman disappeared around a corner and reappeared carrying two bags.

Camille thanked him in Italian with a big smile. She glanced down at her bags, and then up at Michael. "That one's full of my makeup and jewelry, and you know, the important things," she said, pointing to the smaller bag. "Please be careful with it, won't you?" She started to walk away from the front desk clutching only her shiny black purse under her arm.

"Are you kidding me?" he said. "You're lugging your own stuff, darling. I'm not your servant." He tugged on the leather strap of his own green case and left her two bags where they lay.

Camille moseyed back to her bags and bending over, said, "All right, but just this one time." Then she followed in his steps, click-clacking in those red high heels of hers.

Chapter Seven

THE RENTAL WAS A RED FIAT WITH A BLACK convertible top. Michael and Camille stared at it as it baked in the scorching sun.

"This?" said Camille as her lovely, big eyes nearly burst from their sockets.

"Dammit!" barked Michael.

"Maybe they don't have station wagons in Italy. Ever think of that?"

"I don't need to think about any of that right now," Michael snipped, hating the thought that she was probably right.

"So how shall we arrange this?" asked Camille, running her eyes along the fenders to the tiny trunk.

"Again with the we?"

She shrugged.

"I don't know. This thing isn't even big enough for one person's luggage."

A sly grin inched up into one of Camille's cheeks. "I would have to agree, my pet. I wonder where your stuff is going to go."

"Hey, you were the one who wanted to share," said Michael.

Camille set her bags down near the rear of the Fiat and headed toward the front door on the passenger's side. The tiny vehicle had no real trunk to speak of, so Michael squeezed their bags into the back seat. Wiping his brow with a forearm with the back of his hand, he walked around to the front, where he found Camille already sitting in the passenger's seat. "You ready?" he asked.

"Of course," she said, fanning herself with one hand. "I'll drive after the first break."

Michael turned the key in the ignition and adjusted the mirrors. "I thought you said you didn't drive."

"I don't," she replied. "Just trying to keep you on your toes, my darling."

His eyes trailed along the dashboard and over to the glove compartment. "Look in there, would you? See if there's a map. I forgot to ask the girl for one," he said.

"Too flustered by Carlotta's beauty, my darling?" said Camille.

"Just look in the glove compartment, please," he said, with an annoyed sigh. He waited for Camille's reply, and saw her head shake no.

"No map," he said. "What a way to start." He rubbed the sides of his face and his eyes. He twisted at the waist, pulled an old map of Italy from his bag in the back seat and handed it to her. "Looks like you're going to have to navigate using this," he said.

"Hmm?" Camille was really not paying attention. Her mind was on other things. He tried not to think of what they might have been.

"Read the map. Okay?" Michael tapped on the folded map three times with an index finger.

"Oh, all right. I'm good at reading maps," she said. Something told him she was making that up. Set her down in the middle of Manhattan or Paris or even London, and she was fine. But the truth was that the woman couldn't find north from south if she had a thousand dollars riding on it. Her sense of direction was based on shopping, not geography. But still, she pressed on. "I'm good at a lot of things."

"I bet," he mumbled.

"What did you say?"

"Nothing." His head flew back and forth as he pretended to adjust the rear-view mirror again. "It's hot. I'll turn on the air conditioning. Okay?" Camille nodded. He searched the panel and pressed the button, but nothing happened. "You have to be kidding me. No air conditioning? We have to drive all the way to Rome with no air conditioning? This just keeps on getting better and better."

"Uh-oh," moaned Camille.

"What's the matter now?" he asked.

"I don't like it very much when I am too hot," said Camille. "And I'm getting hot already." She lifted her red skirt above her knees and exposed a pair of luscious and provocative, milky thighs.

"Yeah. Me, too." He tried to look away, but he couldn't. She used her skirt as a fan for her bottom half. *What nerve she had. How could she?* It just didn't sit right with him that she got to look so devastatingly delicious right now. In fact, it seemed to Michael already that a few too many things didn't sit right. Camille was making an impression on him, though he couldn't define what kind. And that was the last thing that he wanted.

With the convertible roof firmly fastened to the rear, the windows rolled down, and the map in Camille's hand, the little red Fiat pulled away from the curb. They were off! For the first few kilometers, the grey and brown concrete buildings with graffiti-strewn walls dominated both sides of the narrow highway that led them out of Naples. But after a few minutes ride beyond the city, the travelers had some breathing space and a view of a breathtaking landscape. Picture-perfect patchwork of greens, browns, reds and oranges dotted the countryside along with ancient stone and brick houses. Vineyards arranged themselves neatly on sloping hills, bell towers soared into the sky, and the occasional dairy farm or old barn displayed its idle cows and sleepy sheep. The land was dry—its dust was beaten down by the scorching Mediterranean sun. And the hot wind did little to comfort the mismatched pair as the tiny car chugged along.

Camille gazed off out her side of the red Fiat as they rode along in silence. She spotted a medieval castle up ahead, atop a long hill in the distance. Glad for the distraction, she cried,

"Michael, look! A castle! And it's a big one! I have to take pictures. I just have to. Please, can we stop?"

"Did you just call me 'Michael'?" he asked, twisting his head to face her.

"Did I? I don't think so," she said. A wedge appeared in her brow, and just as quickly, it vanished.

"Oh, please, can we stop? Please?"

"Why not?" he said. "I'm about ready for a drink. Maybe they have some good, old-fashioned, Italian wine."

"Wine? At this time of the day?" she asked.

"Sure," he said. "Something wrong with that?"

She held up her hands, scrunching back in her seat. "I guess not," she said because deep down she was thinking how a little wine sounded pretty good right about now. She turned and uttered softly, "Thanks for stopping, Michael."

The enormous sun began its arching descent towards the bountiful hills. The travelers turned off the A1 highway, where the Romanesque tower loomed large in the distance. Standing alone at the top of the highest hill in the region, the huge stone fortress took up their entire plane of view. The Fiat creaked up the winding road to the front entrance, and before the tiny car had even come to a complete stop, Camille jumped out. She forced the little door open and flew out in a mad dash to click away at her camera, without noticing that she had torn her skirt on the door. She danced around the high walls of the sandstone fortress, clicking and flashing with her camera, then gaily humming in her own little photographic world.

Michael observed her for a time, trying to comprehend the degree of attraction she felt. Was it the castle, or the camera, that mesmerized her so? Either way, she seemed like a little girl to him. Giddy and gay, and innocently playful, like the cute female playmates he now recalled from way back in elementary school. He allowed her to shoot the grey walls against the darkening sky until finally, the camera fell to her waist. Panting, she neared him. Her whole face was beaming. "Okay?" he asked, nodding.

She exhaled heavily. "Very okay," she said.

"Come on. Let's see who's home."

Michael swung the brass knocker on the tall wooden door. It slammed hard against the old wood, echoing like a distant thunderclap. As they waited, all was still. Camille looked up, unable to see the top of the soaring stone tower. Michael walked around to the right side of the building, but soon returned sullenly to the front door. He banged the knocker again against the weighty door, and this time, it slowly creaked open.

A chubby, blonde woman of about sixty-five years appeared behind it, wearing a pale-blue cotton dress hemmed at the knees and a pink cardigan. *"Si?"* she asked. But when she noticed that they were travelers, she perked up. "Come in, come in! Welcome! Do you have the reservation?"

"Reservation? What for?" asked Michael.

"This is Montesole Castle Hotel," the woman answered, with a sweeping gesture. "You need the room for tonight, *si?*"

She looked at them directly, smiling in a confident beam. Montesole Castle dated back to the early twelfth century. The castle and its surrounding city had seen its fair share of medieval battles and sieges. Now, restored and masterfully transformed into an impressive Italian bed and breakfast, the stunning castle served as a lovely rest stop for travelers through the Italian countryside.

Michael and Camille faced one another and shrugged. "It seems like a nice place," he said, "but we're on our way to Rome. We just stopped to take a few pictures."

"Nice? It's gorgeous!" cried Camille. "Look at those columns! And the incredibly high ceiling! And that marble staircase over there!" She gripped the Nikon hanging from her shoulder and pointed it at the staircase.

"You do not need the room?" asked the matron.

"No," he said, "but we'd like to take a few pictures, if that's all right."

"Sure, sure, is okay," said the woman with a smile, "and you eat lunch, yes?"

"Lunch?"

"*Si*. I make amatriciana, the best in Italy. You see." She slipped her pudgy hand around Michael's and tugged.

"I guess we're having lunch here," he said, with wide eyes.

Holding the Nikon out in front of her, Camille snapped the smooth, marble pillars, ancient and mysterious sconces, and intricately carved balustrade. Finally, with a gratifying smile, she indicated that she had finished.

"Come, come," said the woman, "I make the fresh pot of tomato sauce."

"She sounds just like my mother," said Michael.

"I could eat, darling," said Camille. She tucked her camera under her arm and followed them under a high arch into a huge open space that had been renovated into a modern dining room. There were twenty long tables with benches, each one filled with hungry guests who were staying at the hotel or the random passersby like Michael and Camille.

"It seems like they have heard of your amatriciana, too," said Camille.

"*Si. Si*," said the woman. "The best in Italy. I am Angelina Amici. This is my hotel. She is very old and very special. I take good care of her." Angelina had her hands and pointed at a little bit of everything at this ship-shape establishment.

Besides her doorman and front desk duties, Angelina cooked the meals twice a day, handled the guests' laundry, sewed the drapes to her liking, changed the occasional burnt-out light bulb, and unclogged the occasional clogged drain. She wouldn't have had it any other way, no matter how much belly-aching she would hear from her son. He was the General Manager, who reminded her every day of the hard-working staff of thirty which they employed. Anytime he tried to limit Angelina's duties, she would threaten him with a large wooden spoon and remind him of his birthright. She was a remarkable woman who carried a permanent smile around with her, and was dedicated to the castle like it was her masterpiece, a musical symphony or a colossal painting which was babied and caressed, day after day, until a finely polished opus had appeared. Only one thing in her life was more important to Angelina than her bed and breakfast, and that was her family.

"You sit here," she said, pointing Camille and Michael into a small spot barely large enough for one single person on the end of one bench. "And enjoy." Then she hopped away like a chubby rabbit around a column to her kitchen.

Chapter Eight

ANGELINA HAD BEEN RIGHT. LIKE EVERY-
one else in the dining room, Michael and Camille loved her amatriciana. In fact, they had loved everything about the lunch. The
full-figured matron had started them off with some artichokes
that had been steamed in white wine and anchovies bathed in
olive oil, binding them nicely with a bottle of pinot grigio. Next,
a smooth, mellow red from Sicily that lingered on the tongue
like a sweet, tart, plum-cherry juice accompanied fried calamari,
roasted peepers, and grilled porcini mushrooms. Then a deep
rich Chianti, which warmed every fiber of their insides, comple-
mented a big bowl of Angelina's famous spaghetti all' amatriciana, its pancetta and onions taunting their nostrils. A childhood
playmate of Angelina's who now lived in Tuscany had brought
two cases of the Chianti to the castle. Michael had raved about
its depth and body, so much so that Angelina ceased her mini

wine tasting class and kept on pouring the Chianti. By the time they had finished the meal, the two guests from New York were swooning.

Rounding their table after checking on her other guests, Angelina stopped in front of them and placed her arm around Camille's shoulder. "I think you need the room now," she said, winking at Camille.

"I think you're right," said Camille.

She grasped her arm around Angelina's full waist and turned to face Michael. "Now go fetch our bags, my pet."

Michael jabbed a finger at her perfectly straight nose. "I told you before, I'm not your servant, but this one time, I guess I'll…oh, never mind." He stood and stumbled back through the lobby and then back to the red Fiat.

A few moments later, Michael came bounding through the massive doorway with the three bags. As he saw Camille and Angelina approaching, Michael said, "Here you go, Your Highness," and left the red suitcase and her makeup and jewelry bag lying in the middle of the foyer. He wiped the sweat from his brow and tugged on his green case with his nose in the air. A harrumph from Camille was the only reply. But Angelina was smiling to herself.

The chatty, chubby woman led them to the long, polished counter and handed them a small registration card. Camille took up the card and said, "Oh, I'm sorry. There's only one card, and we need two rooms."

Angelina breathed in a short breath, threw her hands up just below her throat, and replied, "*Mi dispiace*. But we have only one room available tonight."

"What do you mean?" asked Michael.

"Montesole, she is...how you say...being fixed," said Angelina.

"You mean renovated?" asked Camille.

"*Si, si*. Renovate, she is renovate now, so, only one room. I am sorry," explained Angelina. With hopeful eyes, she added, "But, your room, she is *bella, molto bella*." She brought her hand to her pink lips and kissed the tips of her pudgy fingers.

The travelers stared at each other in a silent debate. Knowing he had consumed too much wine to continue the drive, Michael shrugged. Camille, herself in no condition to go one mile further, even though she would just be in the passenger's seat. So she turned to Angelina and said, "Okay."

"*Meraviglioso*!" cried Angelina. She brought her hands together in a thunderous clap. "I will show you now. *Venga*, come." She led them up a white, marble stairway to the second floor, and down a long, wide, hallway with extremely tall and exquisitely carved, wooden doors on either side. Hand-carved, painted door plaques, which no doubt had been crafted by Angelina as well, hung from every door. The sparkling woman opened the door to Room 207 and handed them the key. It was the old-fashioned skeleton kind that had been hooked on a long slab of rubber embellished with the hotel's insignia, which depicted the sun inching over the hills of an older Italy.

Michael held out a ten thousand lira note and said, "Thank you."

"I cannot take that," said Angelina. "I do this because I love her." She raised her hands and head, and swept the walls with loving eyes. "Dinner, she is at eight. I think you like. Is *melanzana*. Eggplant. Everyone like my eggplant." The cheery matron ushered the two inside their room and then escaped back down to her kitchen.

Inside, the room was a cozy terracotta brown. Its stone walls and four bedposts extended upward to a nondescript grey-blue ceiling. An antique vanity sat quietly opposite the high bed and a maroon leather chair and matching sofa were positioned off to one side. On a far wall was a stone fireplace, and its embers from the room's last occupants were in a small pile in the center. Camille dropped her purse and camera on the bed and peeked into the bathroom. "It has a pretty shower. Do you mind if I go first, darling?" she asked, examining the newly-remodeled bathroom. A white toilet and oversized sink shared the space with a cylindrical, clear glass booth accented in sleek stainless steel. The young woman eyed the long, lean control panel that activated the shower and steam bath, finding it nearly impossible to wait another second to feel the water on her skin.

"Go ahead," answered Michael. "I can keep myself busy."

She skipped over to the bed, hoisted her red suitcase on top, opened it, and removed a fresh black dress. "Turn away," she said, noticing he was watching from the oversized, leather chair.

"Why? You got a bomb in there?"

"Just do it, my darling. I don't want you seeing my under-things." Her hand was hidden inside the case.

"Honey, I've seen under-things before," Michael said.

"Not mine you haven't," answered Camille. "And darling, you never will."

"You don't know me very well, do you?"

She raised a finger at him. "Now, now."

"All right," he said, turning away.

She pulled a pair of silver lace panties from her case and held them in one hand under her blouse. With the other, she laid the dress out on the bed, tip-toed into the bathroom and locked the door behind her.

She set the clean panties on the toilet seat cover and tore her blouse over her head. With lightning speed, she reached behind her back, unfastened her brassiere, and unzipped the red skirt, letting it fall to the floor along with her panties. She noticed the small tear in the skirt and wondered how it had happened, then chuckled over the grass stains. Camille slid open the rounded door, stepped in, and quickly pushed a button on the panel. The steamy water cascaded down her shoulders and she immediately melted from its soothing touch. She let the pulsating droplets beat against her aching muscles for a minute or two before greedily lathering up. The young woman caressed her white skin with a touch as soft as a lover's, savoring each gentle stroke until she lost herself to the rich lather, forgetting the cares of the outside world. After rinsing off, Camille activated the steam, allowing her pores to breathe in the radiating warmth. Then she touched another button on the silver control panel and the soothing shower ceased. Camille stepped out a new woman, ready to take on the world once again.

On the other side of the bathroom door, Michael was unpacking a long-sleeved white shirt, a pair of black trousers, and a fresh pair of black underpants. He tossed everything on the bed, and then quietly paced over to the bathroom to check that the water was still running. Back at the bed, he nearly peeked inside Camille's red case, but the thought of toying around with her delicate panties stopped him. He unzipped her makeup and jewelry bag instead. Peeking in and around the small bag, he found a white three-ring binder under a collection of perfume bottles. He pulled the binder closer and opened it. It was filled with Camille's photographs. Landscapes, portraits, and a few city scenes of New York. Some were color and some were monochrome, but all of them looked like they had been shot by a professional.

Just then, the knob on the bathroom door began to turn. He jabbed the binder back into the bag and pulled on the zipper. Camille eased out of the bathroom wearing a white bath towel over her silver panties. She tucked the towel in tightly above her breast, suspiciously eyeing him as he dashed over to the comfortable leather chair. He sat for a second to hide his guilt, then started for the bathroom.

Once Michael was behind the door, Camille approached the bed, dropped her towel and slipped into the short black dress. Running her fingers through her damp hair, she examined his clothes, and then her makeup bag, wondering what he would think if he ever looked inside. Would he be able to see her as the down-to-earth southern girl she had once been before? Or would he only see the chic woman bedeviled by the big city? She held her hand at her mouth, not believing herself how much she had changed.

She slid into the vanity chair and examined her perfect features in the old mirror. Her questioning eyes stared back at her, and she looked into the depths of her grey-green pools as if she were spiraling to an abyss. She stroked the supple skin on her face and applied a soft dusting of makeup, and then strode over to the bathroom door and knocked. It was slightly ajar and she wedged it a bit further, peeked her head in, and called, "Darling?"

"Yeah?" an irritated Michael yelled back. Shampoo covered his scalp and ran into his squinting eyes.

She remained behind the white door and called, "I'm going downstairs to look around a bit, okay?"

"Okay," he spat, over the running water.

"I'll meet you in the dining room. Don't dilly-dally, my darling."

"How can I finish if you keep interrupting me, my pet?" he shouted. "Go already!"

"I'm going," she chimed back.

Michael washed all over and rinsed, quickly ending the shower. With a plain white towel wrapped around his waist, he left the bathroom and immediately walked over to the bed. He eyed her small case again, wondering if a second look at that mysterious binder would be worth the risk.

Chapter Nine

DINNER WAS EVEN WILDER THAN LUNCH. It started at eight o'clock and didn't finish until nearly eleven. Angelina's eggplant was a hit with the guests, but it was just one dish amongst many that titillated the taste buds in the crowded dining room. There were sliced meats and hunks of cheeses from several regions of Italy, pastas like bucatini and tagliatelle, mussels and shrimp, beef, lamb, and rabbit, and others with names Michael and Camille could never remember if they tried. It was a wonder, Michael commented, that the B&B was making any money at all. Three nonstop hours of eating came to an uproar when one intoxicated guest had made a seductive overture to another guest, who was incidentally, not in the same party as the drunk. The man brushed up a bit too close for comfort to the woman, and she smacked him "good across the face," as she had later put it. The blow made him swirl and spin, and then topple to the floor. Angelina used good judgment bringing the dinner festivities to a close right after that.

Seeing his opportunity, Michael lifted a half bottle of Chianti from the table where he and Camille were sitting, and said to her, "Let's go."

"Agreed," she replied.

He pulled out the bench and she stood. Swinging the bottle of wine, Michael threw his arm over Camille's shoulders, and the two tipsy Americans slid away from the commotion of the dining room and then down three stone steps that led out into the castle gardens. The smell of lavender and rose filled the air as they meandered along a gravelly path lined with tall cedars and elms under an orangey full moon. Michael stopped at an old stone bench. "Come on, let's sit a while." He thumped the bottle down on the weathered stone seat.

Camille half sat, and then set a finger on the tip of his nose. She quickly stood. "Oh, no you don't. I see what you're doing here."

"What? I'm not doing anything. Just taking a break, you know, from all the action in there."

"No, you're not," she said, jabbing a finger into his shoulder. "You're going to try to get me to sit on this bench. Then talk about how delicious dinner was. We'll sip the rest of this bottle of wine with you, and you'll get me to look up at the lovely moon. And then, darling..."

"I'll do all that?" he asked, thinking that that sounded like a pretty good plan, even if it wasn't his.

"Yes," she answered. "And then, we'll pretend I'm not...." She stumbled on her heels, reaching for the armrest, and Michael caught her by the arm as she landed on the stone seat. "Whew, that was close. Good thing I was here to save you," said Camille, a sizeable hiccup escaping from her pouty lips.

"Yeah. Good thing."

"What's the word? What's the word?" she blubbered. "Pretend I'm not..." She blew a frustrated whoosh through vibrating lips.

"Engaged?" he offered.

"That's it," she said. "What...what you said there, engaged." She started to slide down along the grey stone, her spine curving into a half circle as her head drooped toward her chest. She lifted her chin and let out a labored sigh, then waved her hand around aimlessly. "I had a little wine, and the moon, and the... you're going to think I forgot, aren't you, darling? And then remind me of how very charming you are with this full moon, in this bright starry sky." She sighed. "Why did you think I forgot? I didn't forget. Why did you think that? About the moon, and the wine, how very romantic it all is? That's right, that's right. I didn't forget, you know. That I won't be able to, um, resist you. Yeah, that's it, isn't it? Well, let me tell you, mister..." She exhaled sharply and pointed a limp finger at him. "I forgot." A lengthy silence with more heavy breathing, and her hand fell to her lap. "There. I told you."

"You certainly did," said Michael, chuckling to himself.

"And now I suppose you're going to make me...you know..." She spun her finger around in circles.

"I do?" He searched her eyes intently.

Camille leaned in close to his face, tapped his lips playfully and said, "Kiss you, my pet. That's it." She exhaled. "Well, I've seen a lot of those romantic-ky kinds of movies, my sweet."

He chuckled, his eyes telling her that it wasn't such a bad idea, but his lips said, "I wouldn't dare." He looked at her curiously. She was cranky and demanding when she was hot, tough and brave when she was challenged, and spunky and adorable when she was drunk. He wondered, *am I falling for her, or is it just the wine and the moonlight?*

Camille backed away. "Just as well. You Italians don't know anything about kissing anyway." She lifted heavy arms and they flopped back down in her lap.

He snorted a chuckle. "Come on. Break's over," said Michael. He stood, helped her to her feet, and took a swig from the bottle. He peered at the yellow-orange moon, paused for a brief half moment, and said, "Let's go." He threw an arm around her shoulders.

She slowly lifted his hand off her shoulder and held it at arm's length like it were a dirty diaper, and finally, let it fall. "I can manage," she said. He backed away with his hands held up.

Climbing back up the three stone steps, Camille peeked up at the full moon and tripped on her heels in quite an unla-dylike way, She nearly tumbled over before latching onto his forearm. He heaved her through the large, airy entranceway and they wobbled arm in arm up the semi-circular marble stairway.

Once inside their room, Camille instantly fell back onto the bed. Michael paid her little mind as he started burning the wood in the fireplace. He then glanced over at the bed. Camille was sprawled out on top of the ivory bedspread. He watched her for a long while, until he could hear nothing but a soft, sweet rustling of summer fronds through the open window.

Then, from her position lying in the bed, Camille said, "Dinner was really lovely, don't you think?" When he didn't answer, she sat up on the bed.

"Feeling better?" he asked.

"Yes, thank you," she replied. She skidded off the edge of the high bed and strolled over to her suitcase, which was propped up on a stand in front of the closet. Camille paused briefly, glanced over at Michael, then drew a pale pink night-gown from the case. "I have to change. Wait outside."

"I will not," he replied flatly.

"Then go in the bathroom," she said, holding the night-gown up to her chest.

"*You* go in the bathroom. I'm comfortable," he said, squiggling around in the leather chair.

"I don't want to," she answered, unsure why she was being so despondent. She took a moment for a bothersome sigh and added, "At least close your eyes."

"I can do that." He slowly lifted one hand toward his face.

"How do I know I can trust you?" she asked, eyeing him suspiciously, her head on a slant.

"After what we've been through, my pet?"

"All right. But I'm warning you," she said, pointing a finger. "You better have them closed."

Michael slapped one hand to his face in an exaggerated manner, then the other. "One Mississippi...two Mississippi..."

"Cut that out."

The soft rustle of the silkiness of the black dress slipping over her shoulders and head haunted him. His manly instinct to gaze at the soft material divorcing itself from her supple ivory skin battled his better judgment. But he held on, savoring the sweet sound and smell, if not the sight.

She slipped on the pink nightgown, hung the black dress in the closet, and tip-toed on naked feet back to the bed. "Okay. You can open them now."

She was everything he had envisioned without his eyes, her womanly figure a soft silhouette created from the moon beams striking ancient stone and bouncing through the window pane into the room. He stole a fast glance before she hopped up on the bed and pulled her calves under her thighs. It was all that was needed to imprint her curvaceous womanly figure through the translucent nightgown on his brain. Michael lifted himself from the chair and joined her on the bed.

He lay staring at the dark, high ceiling, not thinking about his Italian half-brother, but only about her. He wanted to stop wasting his time on thoughts of her and just sleep, but he couldn't. Her quirky laugh and honey sweet smell seeped into his pores and down to his very soul. She made him laugh and made him scream, and tortured him with the memory of her shapely figure in that nightgown. Firmly imprinted on his mind were her curves, her long, supple, alabaster limbs, her perfect nose, her cute crooked grin. It was infuriatingly adorable — all of it, all of her. It was all he could do to put it out of his mind.

"Michael, my pet?" she whispered.

"Yes?"

"Good night."

She turned away from him and onto her side, her eyes wide and fully opened.

"Good night," he whispered, "my darling."

It was a very long silence that followed, until the two of them finally drifted off to sleep.

Chapter Ten

THE NEXT MORNING, WHILE MICHAEL LAY sleeping, Camille tip-toed over to his olive-colored case and pulled out a tattered notebook. When she opened the book, a host of addresses and roughly-sketched maps, and a collection of photos and papers spilled onto the floor. She glanced over to the bed. His slow and steady breaths reassured her that the noise didn't wake him. She looked at the book again. His notes were a perplexing puzzle with many missing pieces. Up until that point, she hadn't really believed his story about a missing half-brother. But this new evidence made her think twice. *Why was I so suspicious anyway?* she wondered. Deep down, she felt it wasn't in her nature to act this way. Did she become like this over time? She always had been a good girl growing up in the deep south. She was kind, considerate, and always put others before herself with a smile that could light up a small city. What was it that made her change, this sweet little girl, into a suspicious woman?

She heard movement coming from the bed, quickly stuffed the notebook back into his suitcase and dashed into the bathroom. "I'm in the bathroom," she called to him. "I'll be right out." She flushed the toilet and ran the water in the sink. She gazed at herself in the mirror, smudging away the guilt. Then she patted her cheeks, ran a quick brush through her hair, and took a deep breath before heading back out. She saw that Michael was still groggy and was stretching his limbs. "Oh, you're awake. How did you sleep, my sweet?" she asked.

"Just great," he said, clearing his throat.

"Me, too. I feel so rested," said Camille. "What a marvelous bed. Too bad you had to sleep on your side, darling, away from the window, where all the marvelous moonlight came through."

"Yeah, too bad," he said, with a grin.

"Well, I feel marvelous. I haven't had a sleep that well in a long time." Camille stretched her arms up above her head and let them fall in a circle. She was not able to recall anything from her dreams but was still left with a blissful feeling. She wished she could have remembered them, because during the night, her mind had drifted to a faraway land where tall cypress trees swayed in the supple summer wind. She had clung to a tree trunk and then spun around its base with a childlike innocence, looking out at the fields of bright red roses and poppies that stretched on forever. Without a care in the world, she basked in this splendor, allowing herself to be swept away. Her tranquil delight had morphed into energized passion when a confident Michael in dashing medieval garb neared her on a striking white unicorn that mysteriously transformed itself into a gigantic white limousine with feathery wings. As the magical vehicle-beast approached, Michael leaned over its side and swept her up in his arms. He pressed his lips to hers and they rode off into an intoxicating setting sun.

When Camille began moaning in her sleep, Michael had sat up and turned from his side of the bed to check on her. He leaned over her and waited. She was on her back, and her face seemed like it was glowing in the luminescence of the moonlight. Her breathing slowed as her breast steadily and serenely heaved up and down. He fought the urge to land a silent kiss on her glowing cheek, and then in the next moment, he could've sworn he had heard her whisper his name.

"How nice for you, my pet," he said.

Camille ambled over to the mirror opposite the bed and checked her face and hair. "I'm hungry this morning," she said. "Are you hungry?" She glanced back at him.

Michael finally sat up. "I have to go to the bathroom."

"I wonder if that was a yes," she said, smirking as he walked away.

She began humming from a sweet child's lullaby, then paused as he made his way into the bathroom. "I wonder what Angelina's cooking up in the kitchen," she called to him. But Michael didn't hear. "She's an amazing cook, don't you think? I mean, last night, her dishes were monumental. I never tasted anything like it."

Michael flushed the toilet and jumped in the shower, letting the soothing water splash over his body. He scrubbed his face and hair clean, trying to forget that she was on the other side of the bathroom door. After a quick wash and rinse, he was soon toweling off. He looked in the moirror. He was beginning to resemble himself, so he emerged from the bathroom with a white towel wrapped around his waist. Drying his hair with a smaller towel, he said, "I couldn't hear you. What did you say?"

"I said last night's dinner was something," said Camille. She turned away from the mirror and faced him. He stared at her and thought how the young southern belle from New York looked like she belonged in Europe. Her lavender skirt accented her shapely hips magnificently, and its sharp pleats fell to the length of the garment. The pale-pink, sleeveless blouse she had chosen allowed the breath of morning to linger on her supple white limbs. She smoothed the long, silky strands of hair that flowed freely down her back like black, like liquid mercury. Her eyes were shining with a newness Michael hadn't seen before.

"Yeah, I guess so," he said. "Last night was something." Unable to fight the power of her eyes, his stare became glued to the raven-haired beauty. He gawked at her, mouth gaping, unable to bring his thoughts to an honest finish.

Camille eyed Michael greedily as he stared without blinking. The poor fellow—his lust for her was seeping through his naked pores. He'd even forgotten that he had to slide over to his suitcase for fresh clothes. "You look like a dog at supper-time," she said. Passing him as she crossed the room, Camille propped up his drooping chin with the back of her hand. "Meet you downstairs, my pet," she added, making quite sure he would witness the exaggerated sway of her womanly hips as she headed out of the room.

Descending the marble staircase, Camille expected to see Angelina at one of her posts—the front desk, the laundry room or the kitchen. But instead, she spotted a tall slender man of about twenty-five coming from the kitchen. He wore a bright, lemon-yellow, long-sleeved dress shirt. The crisp clean crease of his stark, white pants highlighted his long legs. Handling himself well in English, he introduced himself as "Mario" and ushered her to a table in the dining room. He told her he was studying fashion design in Paris, but was now home for the summer holidays. Mario lent a hand at the castle hotel whenever he could to pick up extra cash for school tuition and other essentials.

Mario pointed and Camille peered out through the huge window to the sun-drenched terrace. Her mouth went agape. There was Angelina playfully avoiding eye contact with a tall, muscular man of about her age. With a shy smile, she was half leaning, half sitting on the stone wall that separated them from a sea of Italian cypresses and chestnut trees. During what seemed like some sort of youthful flirting game, the burly man knelt in front of Angelina and presented her with a single red rose. Camille gazed at the couple and asked, "Mario, who is that tall man with Angelina?"

"That is her husband," said Mario.

Camille cried, "That sneak! She didn't say anything about being married last night." Camille looked up in thought, scratched her chin and shifted her gaze back out through the glass. "I wonder why."

"Maybe because it is a long story," said Mario.

"Is it a love story?"

"*Si*," said Mario.

Camille hugged herself. "With a happy ending?"

"*Si, certamente.*"

"Then I would love to hear it."

"It is a long story," he said. "And I made eggs."

"That's okay," said Camille. "The eggs can wait."

"But you must be hungry," said Mario.

"I don't mind cold eggs."

"I will bring the eggs," Mario said. He started toward the kitchen.

"No, wait." Camille lunged and hooked him by the forearm. "I want to hear what happened first. Please?"

"At least have some juice, miss," said Mario.

"Mario, the story first."

"Okay, like you wish," said Mario. He breathed in long and began. "Many years ago, even before I was born, they fell in love. Angelina was going to marry another man from her village. Angelina's father arranged the marriage for her when she was just a little girl." Mario paused briefly and gazed through the glass at the couple on the terrace. Then the dashing, blue-eyed, young man proceeded to tell Camille about this other man from Angelina's past. He was a man she had never met, and yet she was still expected to marry him. The man's father was a rich farmer, and the son was eyeing a career in business. Angelina's father believed him to be a worthy catch for his daughter. Pleased with himself, he let his wife take care of the necessary wedding arrangements for their daughter to the soon-to-be businessman.

One day, the mother brought Angelina to the town tailor to have her sized for her wedding gown. The fifty-year-old tailor was out running an errand when they arrived. And so a younger man welcomed them, explaining that he was the tailor's son and his father's apprentice. This man's name was Marcello. Marcello was ruggedly handsome with broad shoulders. He had also been blessed with hands like his gifted father's. Mother and daughter were both charmed instantly. Angelina's mother asked if the young man would take her daughter's measurements. Like a world-class musician whose digits lovingly caress the strings of his harp, Marcello's fingers flittered over Angelina's curves ever so slightly as he recorded the numbers in his mind. The young bride-to-be blushed as Marcello's strong, warm hands neared her bosom. By the time the fitting had ended, cupid had spiked them both with his arrow. And it was only a matter of time before Marcello would steal not only the bride away from the entrepreneurial would-be groom, but he would also fabricate the webbing gown with his own two hands.

When they met, Angelina was barely twenty, and Marcello but a year older. But her heart had been pierced strongly, and she knew Marcello would be the only man to ever hold the arrow. Still, out of a deep sense of obligation to her parents and the time-honored tradition, she went along with the wedding arrangements as planned.

But then Marcello made his move. The day before the wedding, he arrived at Angelina's house with the finished gown. When Angelina's parents showed him in, Marcello quickly removed the dress from the garment bag. Then he cocked back his arm with a frightening pair of giant scissors in his hand. The early afternoon's rays bounced dangerously from the shears and Marcello thrust the scissors downward. The onlookers screeched. He jerked his hand away just before it reached the precious garment and threatened to not hold back a second time if Angelina would not be allowed to walk away from the arranged marriage and be his. The young, embarrassed girl stood by, watching in silence as a chaotic quarrel ensued. Her father eventually acquiesced to Marcello's demands. The frustrated father did not understand why his wife had taken Marcello's side from the start, learning only later that she was the sole person who had known of Angelina's secret love for the brawny young man. The following day, Angelina married Marcello. The day was July twenty-second, one month after they had met at his father's shop. And it was of course, the first day of summer.

"So you see," said Mario, "every year on June twenty-second, Angelina and Marcello celebrate that meeting. On that day, they take a little extra time to share their love and remind everyone of how much they mean to each other." He smiled at Camille.

"June twenty-second. That's today!" cried Camille.

"*Essatamente*," said Mario. "Look, they hold hands like young lovers."

All eyes were now peering through the glass out onto the terrace, where the carefree couple sauntered over the terra cotta stones reaffirming their unbreakable love. At that moment, Michael came thumping down the marble staircase in a pair of khaki trousers and a cream-colored, long-sleeved shirt. He spied Camille sitting close to Mario, who to him was a dark, handsome stranger, and then peered through the glass at the couple in love. As he approached Camille, he gestured towards Angelina and Marcello with his nose and asked, "Did they just get married?"

"Oh, you finally decided to join us?" said Camille. "I thought maybe you drowned up there in your own drool, my pet."

Ignoring her remark, Michael said, "So, what's with them?" Then he turned to Mario and pointed at the stranger with a hitchhiker's thumb. "And who's this?"

Camille scoffed and sliced him with a behave-yourself glare. "This is Mario," she said. "He just finished telling me the story of how Angelina and her husband got together. And what a beautiful story it was. So romantic." She paused and sighed longingly. "Too bad you missed it. Maybe Mario can tell it again. You wouldn't mind, would you, Mario?"

The young man shook his head.

"I could hear it again and again. It's such a lovely story." She gazed into Mario's eyes.

The bile in Michael's gut churned. "I think I'll pass," he said, with a gesture to Mario.

"I knew it," said Camille.

"What?"

"I said I knew it."

"Knew what?"

"You're not the romantic type after all."

"Why, because I don't want to hear some sappy love story? I came down for breakfast, not that." He searched the dining area with greedy eyes. "What did Angelina make?"

"Angelina didn't *make* anything," said Camille. "She's got more important things to do today."

"I made eggs," said Mario. "I will go get the breakfast." And the long-legged youth dashed off to the kitchen.

As soon as Mario had gone, Michael stared down Camille and asked, "So what's with this Mario guy? What kind of character is he?"

"What is this, the Italian Inquisition?" she said, searching his eyes. "Wait a minute. Are you jealous?"

"What? No." He felt the heat form on his cheeks.

"You *are* jealous," she said. "This is unbelievable."

"What are you talking about?" asked Michael. He looked down and turned away, mumbling something inaudible to himself, while Camille laughed her awful laugh, the piercing echoes ripping into his soul.

Mario returned with the eggs on two hand-made, ceramic plates which were decorated in a colorful grapevine motif. He also carried a couple of baguettes, some fresh juice, and some coffee. As he dished out his simple breakfast, Camille said, "Hey Mario, listen to this. He's jealous," thumbing the air in Michael's direction. "Can you believe it? He saw us talking, and now he's jealous." But before Mario could respond, she latched onto his forearm and peered into his aqua eyes. Then she quickly thought up another idea. "Hey, wait a minute," she said. "Maybe he's not jealous of *you*, maybe he's jealous of *me*. What a riot." She grinned wide and the tortuous laugh escaped again, after which she faced Michael and said, "Are you gay, my sweet?"

"What! Are you nuts?" he said.

"Then explain why you're jealous of me."

"What are you talking about?" A wedge formed on his brow.

"Didn't you know?" It was all she could do to keep from bursting.

"Know what?"

"Mario," she said, gesturing to the tall man with a nudge of her nose, "he's gay."

Michael's head instantly jerked and he searched Mario's face, the dark handsome man wiggling his thick bushy eyebrows. Shaking his head, Michael buried his eyes behind his hand.

Just then, Angelina and Marcello approached, casually swinging their coiled hands. There was a serene expression on Angelina's face. Camille brought her hands to her breast and tilted her head. "Oh, look at them. They are so in love."

"*Buongiorno*," said Angelina. Her sun-baked glow was still fresh from the mid-morning rays. "You sleep well?"

"Yes, beautifully, Angelina, thank you," said Camille. Michael grumbled an insignificant utterance.

"This is Marcello," said Angelina. "The man of my dreams."

Camille rested a hand on her collar bone, a lump forming in her throat.

Marcello offered a slight bow and said, "*Buongiorno*." He cupped his bride's plump cheeks in his strong hands and whispered to her, "My angel."

Camille fought back tears. "Oh, my," she said softly.

"I go to the garden," said Marcello. "To see Cara. Not long." He stroked his wife's cheek again and his manly fingers trailed off delicately in the warm air.

Angelina smiled at him and nodded. "*Si*. She waits for you."

"Not long," repeated Marcello. He blew his bride a kiss and headed for the garden with a smiling wink.

"Oh, Angelina," said Camille. "I didn't know. He is wonderful. Mario told me the story of how you two met and fell in love. I don't think I've ever heard anything more romantic." Mario's eggs stared up at her in a warning that they would soon turn cold, but Camille was too moved to eat anything.

"*Si, si*. He is a good man. I am very lucky," said Angelina. "*Il Destino.*" She raised her eyes and an index finger skyward.

"Destiny?" asked Camille.

"*Si, il Destino*, she is brought Marcello to me." Angelina slowly twirled in a circle, hugging herself as if in a dream.

Camille gazed at her and said, "Angelina, tell me about your wedding, please?"

"If you are liking, I show you," said Angelina. "Come with me."

"If I am liking?" said Camille. "Are you kidding? Lead the way." Camille stood and looped her lean arm around Angelina's.

"But my eggs," said Mario.

"Oh, I'm sorry, Mario," said Camille. "But I couldn't eat a thing right now. I'm just too excited." The two ladies hurried away from the dining room, abandoning a hungry and grumbling Michael and a pleased-with-himself Mario who was primping his lemon-yellow collar. In passing, Angelina hugged herself as she and Camille peeked through the large framed window. Her beloved Marcello was out in the garden chasing after his five-year-old granddaughter with a tape measure.

In her second floor bedroom, Angelina walked over to the far wall and tugged on a thick cord. The weighty, champagne drapes parted, allowing the day's rays to coat the room with warm hues of amber and mustard. The full-figured grandmother drew apart the solid oak doors of a seventeenth-century armoire, its grains glistening and the aged wood creaking softly, to reveal a textile masterpiece. Clutching her breast, Camille gasped. The armoire's only occupant was the wedding gown and it was strung across the chest facing forward. Angelina gazed at the sheathed gown enveloped in a corona of delicate lace and cheek-blush-ing memories of that fateful first day of summer, forty-five years ago, rushed back to her. Playing slowly across her eyes like movie scenes was a lifetime of happiness with Marcello. Arm in arm, the two women dreamed about the same thing, the power of *il Destino*.

Camille sighed. "I wish I could have a gown like that for my wedding," she said.

"You can," said Angelina.

"Oh, no, I can't," said Camille. "I already have a different one."

"Oh, my dear, you engaged?" said Angelina. "Wonderful! I know you and Michele will be so happy together. Like me and my Marcello." She threw her pudgy arms around Camille and pulled her close. Releasing her grip, the matron stroked Camille's cheeks with both hands.

"No, no, no. Not Michael," said Camille. She grasped Angelina by the wrists. "I'm going to marry a different man named Claude. He's in Paris. He is my one true love."

Angelina pulled away and peered intently at Camille. Stone-faced, the normally cheery Italian woman had a single word for the young American: "Oh."

Chapter Eleven

TWO CHILDREN AND THEIR SPOUSES, FIVE grandchildren, and thirty hotel employees had joined Angelina and Marcello in the celebration of the day. An additional twenty or so friends had dropped by for the festivities, as was the custom in the region. Young men in brown suits lightly strummed mandolins and waiters in sharp, white jackets trotted around the garden with mounds of finger food on shiny, silver platters. Delighting the guests were appetizers of beef carpaccio and prosciutto di Parma, buffalo mozzarella and parmagiano reggiano, anchovies, and olives. And there was enough wine to quench the parched throat of Bacchus. The first day of summer came but once a year, and the joyous couple never wasted one precious minute of it. They spared no expense, welcoming the newcomers from America the same as all the rest.

Camille dropped a mini ball of mozzarella into her mouth, chewed silently, and swallowed. "I'm so glad Angelina's happy," she said. "I love a happy ending." She accented a melancholic sigh. "Such a lovely story." She glanced at Michael. "Didn't you think it was lovely?"

"I guess," he said, too involved with the hors d'oeuvres to fully consider it.

"You guess?" she said. "Come on. It was her sweetheart, and they fell in love at first sight. True love! You guess." She shook her head and took a small sip of champagne.

Michael shrugged, gobbled down a hunk of carpaccio, and flung back his champagne.

Camille caught him peeking at the happy couple, tapped on his chest, and said, "I know there's a heart in there somewhere." She nodded. "Look at them, would you? Childhood sweethearts. Don't you remember yours?" When he offered no comment, she added, "Ah, come on, don't be shy. You know who your sweetheart was.

"I really didn't have one," he said, now munching on a bit of cured ham.

"What? What is the matter with you?" she said. "No childhood sweetheart? Everyone has a sweetheart from their youth. At least, they should." And this got her thinking about her own, how she had met him in her senior year of high school on a class trip to Paris. He had been wonderfully charming and dashing. He was tall, dark, smooth-talking, and romantic, and he had won her heart almost instantly. They'd watched God-beaming sunsets through the multi-colored glass at Sainte-Chapelle, ad taken carefree strolls along the Ponts des Arts, and had watched lazy tour boats glide down the Seine. They had romanced the languid nights away, whispering sweet nothings until the wee hours of the Parisian morning.

A short waiter with a thick, purple-black, curly mop of hair happened by with a tray full of shrimp. Camille daintily lifted one, dipped it into the cocktail sauce, and eased it into her mouth in a very ladylike manner.

"I did like this one girl," said Michael. He quickly turned his face away and stuffed his mouth with two shrimp he had grabbed from the same silver tray.

"See? I was right. Everyone has one," said Camille, poking the same finger into his chest. "Even you."

"All right. That's enough." He batted her made-for-piano fingers away, and brushed the front of his shirt. "She wasn't my sweetheart," said Michael. "I mean," he lowered his eyes, "I wanted her to be. I liked her, a lot. But we never got together. I think I was just too shy."

"You, my pet? Shy?"

He snorted a chuckle with no other reply.

"What was her name?" asked Camille, holding her champagne flute up to her lips.

"Kim. Kim Kruger. She was from a strict German family." His mind floated back, and it was 1957 all over again, in September, in New York. The fourth grade had just begun and there she was, ten-year-old Kim Kruger, the love of his very young life. The shy and sweet little girl with bright pink, clown cheeks and fine, blonde hair that she wore, long to her hips. Other days, she'd clip it back and away from her innocent, young face with a tortoise shell barrette. Camille watched him as his inner child's smile now covered his manly face. As the sweet soul of youth washed over him, he was sure he could reach out and touch the hem of young Kim's light green skirt.

"How old were you? Sixteen, seventeen?" asked Camille.

"Almost ten," he said, very quickly, and tore off a big piece of ham and cheese sandwich with his teeth.

"Ten?" she said. "Oh, I bet you were a real heartbreaker at ten. Poor little Kim Kruger, never stood a chance, did she, my sweet?" Camille tore at his memories with her notorious cackle.

"Hey, I'll have you know, I really was in love," he said, still chewing away at the bit of sandwich. Michael's brows formed a deep wedge. What did this pest of a woman know of his childhood or of what he had felt at that tender young age? He wondered if Camille had been born snooty, never having known the pure innocence of youth. Maybe she'd never had the freedom from anonymous inhibitions.

"I'm sure you were," said Camille, nodding with a snide grin. "Michael, the heartbreaker." She grinned again. "I just could never imagine that anyone would ever admit to being in love at such a young age."

"What about you?" he said. "I can just picture it. Lovely little Camille in her blue and white Saint Mary's uniform, skirt flapping in the brisk autumn breeze. And snooty you, rejecting each and every boy-man suitor as he tried to take his place in the ranks. Poor little guys, doomed before ever going into battle." He shot her a nasty smirk and she challenged it with a stink eye, but said nothing. His breathing calmed. "So, did you have one?" he said, after a calming pause.

"One what?" she said, but with a certain reluctance. Her arms were folded tight against her torso, like she was trying to hide her breasts. Or her ego. It was like she was embarrassingly covering the fact that she was a perfectly-formed, sensual woman who had been torturing the opposite sex since the age of ten.

"Childhood sweetheart."

"Of course," she said. Annoyed only a moment, she quickly wore a smile. "I'm marrying him at the end of the summer. So put that in your pipe and smoke it."

"I'm sorry," said Michael. *What else could I say?* he wondered

"What for?" she said. "I'm very happy with my Claude. I can't think of anyone I'd rather be with. He's tender and smart. And he cares a great deal about me and my hopes and dreams for the future. I'm a very lucky girl. I found Claude when I was very young. He was my first love, and my true love. The best kind of love. What more could a girl ask for?" The words were straightforward enough, but there was something in her tone and her redundant nature that smacked of insecurity. She was reaching out for something, or someone. It was like she had a question and she was lunging for someone to help her with the answer.

"Yes, of course. The best kind," he said.

"Are you mocking me?"

"I would never," he said, and raised his hands like he was being held at gunpoint. "He sounds like a great guy. Tall, funny, smart. Probably rich, too."

"You *are* mocking me," she said. "How dare you!"

Now that was straightforward, thought Michael.

She folded her arms and hid her breasts again. "How dare you presume that I don't love Claude! Just who do you think you are?" Her big, round cat eyes narrowed now. If she were a dragon, flames would have been bursting from those pulsating nostrils. "You don't know me. You don't know anything about me. Or my Claude."

"I never said I believed you didn't love him," said Michael. "I think *you* believe you love him. And I'm sure he really is tall, smart, and handsome. I don't doubt that. But he's just not the right guy for you."

By all accounts, why shouldn't she have been in love with Claude? *He really is all the things a woman hopes for,* she thought. "You insolent pig!" she said. "Where do you get off saying that about my fiancé?"

"Whoa. Insolent pig." His eyes nearly popped out of their sockets. "That's going a bit too far, wouldn't you say?"

"No, I wouldn't," she said. "And anyway, look who's judging me." She paused, thinking she had been too easy on him. "You've got a lot of nerve, you know that, mister?"

He jabbed a thumb into his chest with a whispered, "Me?"

"And I suppose you've got it all figured out," said Camille. "The ten-year-old heartbreaker has got it all figured out."

"You know what?" said Michael. "Can we just drop it? I mean, all of it. I'm already tired. And I haven't even started the engine."

"You tire me, too," she said, and looked away.

But little did they know just how exhausting the next leg of their journey would be.

Chapter Twelve

AFTER SAYING GOODBYE TO ANGELINA, Marcello, and Mario, the travelers loaded their luggage into their red Fiat. They put the black convertible top down and began the remainder of the drive to Rome. The road they were traveling was a simple one with easy curves. And on either side of it there were hills of grape vines as far as the eye could see. The idyllic landscape was dotted with the occasional farmhouse and barn, or church with its spire lurching skyward. Cows, goats, and pigs were also present, making it a comforting setting for the two New Yorkers.

The sun bore down hard on their little, red workhorse. It was an empty and hot roadway, and Camille was becoming cranky again. She leaned over her door warding off the stifling effects of the heat and a blast of hot air rushed into her face.

She pulled herself back over the seat and flipped open the map, silently calculating distances and times. "You know, if we don't dawdle, we may make it before lunch. Rome doesn't seem that far away."

"No?"

"What do you say?" Her feline eyes were wide with anticipation.

"Sure. We might as well try." He wriggled in his seat and stepped on the accelerator pedal.

A few miles down the road, with Camille studying the map and announcing town names and distances, she was actually starting to enjoy being the navigator. "It looks like we're getting close to the exit. According to the map, it should be coming up soon. Then it's a small road that goes west."

"What small road? What's the number?" he said

"I don't know. Are there numbers on maps?"

"Of course there are numbers on maps."

"Well, not on this one," she said, shaking her head. "There's no number for that road. And no name."

"Just great," said Michael. "I asked for a map. Why'd that rental agent have to be so pretty? It distracted me!"

"See, that's your weakness, my pet. You become putty in the hands of the opposite sex." Camille taunted him with one of her devastatingly annoying laughs.

"Quit joking around, okay?" he said. "We've got to find the road."

"All right. Look, the road heads directly west," she said. "If you get off at the correct exit, you should have no problem getting to Rome." She paused, and a smirk covered her face. "Unless you'd like me to drive."

"No thanks," he said. "I'm not worried about my driving. I'm worried about riding in this matchbox car with a temptress." He peered at the exit sign in the distance, which was about one hundred feet ahead.

"Now that's uncalled for," she said, and slapped him playfully on the shoulder with the map.

"Oh, it's okay when you do it, though," he said, pushing her away with one hand.

"Of course. I'm a girl." She stuck her tongue between pouty lips and blew a raspberry. Michael turned to catch sight of her vibrating tongue before it disappeared back behind her pearly white teeth. He longed for the tongue to flick out at him again. He was just dying to be licked by her.

He turned the Fiat off the highway exiting at the correct place. But that no longer concerned them, because the weather was changing, and for the worse. The sun was swiftly disappearing behind an ominous shelf cloud in the distance.

But he drove on, following that little road which curved and wound, climbing and descending over soft, small hills. With pine and chestnut trees framing either side, the red Fiat chugged along at a steady fifty kilometers per hour. But soon the sun was completely blocked by chunky, silver-black clouds.

"Hey, it's getting dark," said Camille. "How can it be getting dark already?" She glanced down at her watch. "Did I forget to change the time on my watch or something?" The watch read twenty minutes before eleven.

"I don't think it has anything to do with the time," said Michael. He glanced up at the dark, serious sky. They didn't have that much time to ponder it. "Look." He pointed up with his nose, while his hands clenched the wheel. "I'm going to put the top up. Hold on." He didn't bother to pull over and stop. He saw that the rain clouds were speeding toward them with unanticipated quickness. The creaky mechanism bracing the convertible roof locked in place as the wind started to blow hard.

"Uh-oh," said Camille, the fierce dark cloud coming on fast. "That looks serious to me. And it's headed our way, isn't it?"

"I'd say so," he said. "Luckily for you, I know what I'm doing." He forgot everything else and took control. And Camille found herself secretly drawn to that serious and confident side of him.

"I'm not so sure," she said. "In fact, isn't it my turn to drive?" A jagged inflection hinted at her nervousness.

"Just sit quietly while I handle this, sweetheart." He pointed a finger at her seat, like she was a second grader being sent off to the punishment desk.

Camille gave him a mocking salute, and watched him shake his head. Then he bit down on his bottom lip in deep concentration. *Maybe this is more serious than I thought*, she thought.

Loud thunder claps followed screaming bolts of lightning. She knew that her intuition had been right. The crackling thunder turned deafening and the wind kicked up wildly, blowing dark green summer leaves off the branches of the surrounding trees. The storm's howling winds pounded in their ears as the little Fiat revved up for the challenge. "Is your seat belt on?" Michael yelled over the wind and claps of thunder.

"It's on! It's on! You just watch the road!" she yelled back.

"I am." But the narrow road became increasingly harder to see. The drive was wickedly scary, like descending the basement stairs of a haunted house when your candlelight gets snuffed out by a spooky wind. Michael strained his eyes, inching nearer to the windshield. A small tree branch snapped from its trunk and smacked the windshield menacingly and both riders jerking back in surprise. The helpless branch raced over the roof with the fierce driving wind. "Whoa! That was close," Michael said.

Gritting her teeth, Camille jabbed at the air in the direction of the windshield, pointing her finger at the even darker clouds ahead.

A flash of lighting struck a heavier branch, separating it from its trunk. Brilliant light surrounded them, while the branch bounced on and then off the roof. They jumped in their seats, terrified to their cores. Camille shrieked.

Michael reached out to her and grasped her arm. "Hold on! We're going to be all right!"

No sooner had he said when a bolt of lightning struck the car. It flew down from the darkest cloud and blinded them for a full second. When the flash subsided, they turned and looked at each other.

"Are we dead?" he said.

"I don't know. Are we?" Camille pressed her fingers to her face. Then she reached over to Michael's face and held it in both of her hands as she turned him towards her. She searched his eyes. "We're not." She smiled at him and squeezed her palms against his cheeks. "We're alive. I don't know how, but we're alive."

"You must be my lucky charm," he said, now smiling back. He covered one of her hands with his. Then Camille pulled her hands away.

Rain was pounding the car's roof, beginning to accumulate on top so much so that welts were forming and pushing down towards the passengers. The car had stopped dead. Another brilliant flash of light flickered inches away from the car scorching the ground. It left a black hole in the shape of an oval about ten inches long.

Camille shouted, "Do something!"

"I'm trying!" Michael was turning the key in the ignition, but there was no response at all. He yelled over the deafening claps of thunder and howling wind. "It's not working!"

"You get us out of this alive," said Camille, "and I'll forgive you for what you said about me and Claude."

"Deal," said Michael, "but I won't take it back."

"Whatever. Just gets us out of here!"

A few branches broke loose from a nearby hazelnut tree and one flew at the car in the treacherous wind. It landed in the black material roof, near the center, poking its gnarly point right between Michael and Camille. Reacting to instinct, Michael reached up and forced the branch out through the hole. But then the rain poured down inside the car.

"Wonderful!" shouted Camille over the howling wind and pelting rain. "This is much better!"

"Sit still, will you?" he said. He lunged behind him for his leather jacket and stuffed it up into the hole in the roof fabric, abating the falling rain.

Spotting an overhang on the side of the road he cried, "Look! Up ahead! I think we can make it!"

Sandwiched between two large chestnut trees, the rock ceiling covered an expanse of profound darkness that looked like a black hole. The beat-up Fiat, collapsed and in a puddle of muddy rainwater, was not going to make it even to the rock ceiling. Michael turned the key in the ignition one last time, but it was in vain. The Fiat's engine was surely dead. He tore his jacket from the hole in the roof and said, "Come on. Let's go."

They dashed out of the car and started for the ledge. But then Camille stopped abruptly and raced back to the car.

"Where are you going?!" yelled Michael, hovering under his jacket.

"My pictures!" She tore the small bag from the back seat, then turned and raced back to the rock overhang. Michael seemed to be vanishing into the black hole beyond it. What they hadn't seen from their Fiat was that the pitch-black face of this rock ledge was really the entrance to a small cave. There was nowhere else to go but inside it.

Chapter Thirteen

THE CAVE WAS DARKER THAN THE ROAD, but they crept inside until they were out of the storm. Their eyes soon began to adjust to the darkness. The cave was oval-shaped, about three hundred square feet in total size, and contained only the single entrance from which they had entered. But at least they were no longer stuck in the cramped car, being pelted by the rain. They could wait out the storm inside this black hole.

"What were you thinking?" she asked, as soon as their eyes adjusted.

"What? I fixed the roof, didn't I?" he said, whisking the water away from his face with one hand.

"Fixed it?" she said. "You call that fixed? You're insane!"

"Hey, at least I didn't crash."

"No, you almost killed me with a tree branch instead," said Camille. "Thanks a lot."

"Are you crazy?" he said, raising his voice now. "Do you think I planned that or something?"

"I don't know, maybe."

"You're out of your mind, you know that?" He flapped his arms up and down like a drenched duckling.

Camille whisked his gesture away. She unzipped her small case and pulled out her portfolio binder. She let the small case fall to the damp ground and gently opened the binder. "Oh, no!" she said, as raindrops dripped down from the book. "Look at them. They're ruined." She lifted her eyes and glared at him. "It's all your fault."

"*My* fault?" he said.

"Yes. Your fault," she said. "If you knew where you were going, we would have been in Rome before the storm." The anger rose from her belly like molten lava from the earth's core. "You are the unluckiest person I've ever met."

"Me? What about you?" said Michael. "You're the one who was navigating."

"Don't you dare try to put the blame on me," she said. "We're here because you're unlucky. The car with no air conditioning, the tree branch, and now this cave. These things never happened to me before I met you. You've got to be the unluckiest person in the world."

"Is that so?" said Michael. "Well, you're just so... you're so..." His stammering produced nothing; instead, he said, "I never know what you're going to do next. You make me crazy." He wrung his hands.

"I'm tired of all this," said Camille. She waved it away with a gesture of surrender. "What's the difference whose fault it is? My photos are ruined and we're trapped in this cold dark cave." She always hated when things didn't go her way. A storm was an unpredictable and uncontrollable act of nature that infringed upon her routine. She liked things the way she liked them, believing that she could even shape things to her liking. The world was full of the things she could always count on. So being jailed up in this tiny, dank whole in the side of the road, dripping wet and staring at her ruined photos was more than she could bear. "What are we going to do?"

"Come on, it's not that bad," said Michael. He, on the other hand, believed that the universe worked a certain way and that things that were supposed to happen happened. "Besides, we have no choice. We'll just have to wait out the storm. It'll probably be over soon. In the meantime, I'll make a fire. And then we'll dry off those pictures of yours. We'll make it all better. You'll see."

She sighed. Camille could not reconcile the anger and frustration she felt towards him with the ease with which forgiveness swept over her. Something inside her was percolating near the surface, something unusual and something brand new. "I guess you're right. How long can it rain, right?" She set the binder down on the damp floor of the cave and removed her sweater. It left her in only a thin, sleeveless top. Michael tried to remember their predicament as he gazed on her lean, shivering arms and alabaster shoulders.

Michael lifted his leather jacket from his shoulders. He slipped out of his shirt and said, "It's drier than yours." He handed the shirt to her. She told him to turn away, removed her wet top and slipped the shirt over her shoulders. Michael put his jacket back on his naked skin and without a word, began collecting some twigs and leaves. He shaped them into a miniature teepee, pulled a worn brass cigarette lighter from his jacket pocket and made the sign of the Cross. "God, I hope this works," he said. The lighter flickered a small spark only at first, but then the butane ignited, and in a matter of minutes, Michael had a sound blaze going. Next, he lifted a round stone and dropped it near the fire. "Come. Sit," he said, wiping the dirt from the top of the stone. He carried another one over for himself, setting it down across from the first. The flames from the blaze between them began to rise.

Camille could not believe her senses. A few moments ago, she had been terrified. She couldn't see anything, and was cold, soaked to the bone and imprisoned. Now this forbidding world was a different place, a cozy fire softly warming them, its dancing flames casting a healing glow on the walls. Her torso and limbs were drying, she felt more like herself. And inside, she felt safe in Michael's tan shirt. He hopped around the cave gathering more leaves and sticks. He took charge and she liked it, because with great ease he had fixed a major interruption on her routine, and it didn't seem to annoy her anymore. On one hand, she still despised him. But on the other hand, he was some kind of odd magician who could make the bad stuff disappear.

She slipped off her muddy high heels and propped her feet up on a smaller rock, wiggling her toes near the flames. Michael watched her. She was calm. Her breathing had softened and she had settled down comfortably on her stone. He removed his shoes also, then his socks, and waved them at the orange flames. After a while, he set the socks on a rock. "Now, let's have a look at those pictures."

"Oh, what's the use?" said Camille. "They're ruined. There's no fixing them." She sat sulking now, trying to recall the moments when she had taken the photos. She realized that she had placed a memory with each one, and that memory that would disappear along with the ruined images on the photos.

"Let's not be so hasty," said Michael. "Come on, let me see." He wiggled his fingers at her.

Camille passed him the white book and he stared down at its wetness. The first photo was indeed compromised. It was the same photo he had seen in the castle, which featured two young boys, maybe seven or eight years old, with curly, dark brown hair and bubbly smiles playing a game of marbles on a city sidewalk. Camille truly loved that photo. She had taken it with her brand new camera just one week after arriving in New York. The whole idea of a life focused on photography blossomed with those first shots in Manhattan. And because she could not recall what had happened to the negative, she knew the photo was irreplaceable. That hit her hard.

Michael couldn't possibly know how much each picture meant to her, but he flipped through the first part of the album and said in a soft understanding voice, "You know something, there are some really good shots in here." After a short pause where he examined more photos, he added, "You did all this? This is your work?"

She nodded, and said, "What's left of it."

"Oh, come on. It's not that bad," he said. "Look, it's only really the first one that's kind of wet. The rest don't look that bad at all." He held the book out for her, flipping the pages as she reluctantly peeked.

"I don't know," she said glumly with a disgusted shake of her head.

"Well, maybe we can revive the top one," he said, drying it off with his hand. "Look, it's really only the edges that are ruined. I bet you can pass it off as one of those really old photos, those priceless antique ones. Just make believe it's older than it really is." He brushed the photo until it was completely dry, and did the same with the others, and the front and back covers as well. "See? There, good as new. Or should I say old?"

Camille did not respond. The picture had a deep significance which he would never understand, and it was definitely not something she could joke about. The young boys in the photo were not part of Camille's family, were not even friends, just two happy-go-lucky boys she had happened to spot on a sunny, New York, summer day. They hadn't even flinched once as Camille steadied the camera on her tripod and shot various action poses. The photo in her portfolio she held deep in her heart, because the loving expressions on the boys' faces had beckoned a lonely Camille.

Huddling near the blaze, Michael rubbed his hands together. His trousers began to dry while Camille waved her floppy skirt in big swooping movements near the flames. Soon the fire was dying down, so he jumped up and gathered more twigs and leaves. He tossed them on top and gave her a smile, then moved to the cave entrance and saw that the rain was still coming down in sheets. The sky was nearly as dark as the cave. "I don't think we're going anywhere just yet. I'm sorry," he said, returning to his stone seat. She shrugged and let out a sigh.

He watched her again, the way her soft shoulders lifted and fell, the way her ample breasts shifted and swayed, how her mouth puckered into an adorable pout. She was utterly cute and seductive, and he felt he couldn't resist her. "Since we might be here a while, and we have nothing else to do, why don't you tell me what's so great about him anyway?"

"Who?" Her eyes narrowed.

"Mr. Wonderful," he said. "What's his name? I forgot."

"I really don't appreciate your sarcasm," she said. "I've already forgiven you once, since you got us out of the mess which you created. I'm not going to forgive you a second time."

"All right, I'm sorry," he said.

"There you go," said Camille. "That's more like it. And his name is Claude."

"So, my sweet, what's so great about this Claude, that you'd come all the way over here to get married?"

"If you must know," she said.

"I must," he said, raising an eyebrow and shooting her a sly grin.

She moaned a sweet sigh. "He's perfect for me, my pet."

"Perfect?" A small snicker escaped from Michael's lips. "Who's perfect in this imperfect world?"

"Claude is. Just perfect. He knows me," she said. She paused for a moment while she gazed into the flickering orange flames. "He knows when I want to talk and when I need time for myself. He knows when I'm busy with my work and doesn't get in my way. He knows when I want to cuddle, and when I want to—".

"Do the nasty?"

"You see? Right there," she said. "Claude would never say anything like that. He's too refined for that kind of street talk. He's a gentleman, and he's never sarcastic. Or bitter." She opened her cat eyes wide and glared at him.

Michael scoffed. "Sounds like a bore."

"He is not," said Camille. "He's fun, and wise. And he's the perfect gentleman."

This time, with a knowing smirk, Michael laughed hard enough for her to hear.

"What's so funny?" she said.

Michael shook his head. *Perfect. What is perfect?* he thought. *What a mistake, to think anything in life could be perfect.* He reasoned that the reason why she couldn't see her error was because she was on the inside of it—because it was happening to her. It was like when an orator makes a speech. He hears the words coming out of his mouth, but does he understand how he really sounds? Michael sensed that there was something more, something hidden behind that "perfect" that kept her from really living her life. So he asked her, "You want to know what I think?"

"Do I have a choice?"

"I think you're here for a last fling."

"I beg your pardon," she said, backing away with furrowed brows.

Michael swirled the air with one hand. "A last fling," he said, "one for the road."

"What on earth are you talking about?"

Michael shook his head, not believing she couldn't see it. "That's the real reason why you're here," he said, "in Italy, and not in Paris with Mr. Perfect. Your wedding is coming soon. And you know you'll be stuck with him forever. And who really wants perfect, tell me."

"How dare you!"

"That's it, isn't it?" he said. "And deep down, you're afraid."

Camille laughed a short snort and said, "You are dead wrong, my darling. And it's none of your business, by the way, why I'm where I am."

"I don't think so," he said, "I think you're hiding from something. And I think you constructed this Mr. Perfect

Claude in your own mind. He's like the wall that keeps you safe and protected from all the bad and scary things outside, on the other side of the wall. He's a wall to protect you from real life, where it's unpredictable and nasty, unexpected things really do happen."

"You know what I think?" She waited for his reply, but received only a silly smirk. "I think you're out of your mind."

Ignoring her remark, he said, "You're just afraid that without your perfect Claude, you won't know what to do. A perfect man has perfect rules, and you always need to play by the rules."

"And what's so wrong with rules?" said Camille. "A little stability and routine never hurt anybody. Society needs rules. How else are we going to know how to act?" She pulled at the collar of his shirt as perspiration began to bead on her neck. Camille was frightened to consider that he might have been right.

"Don't you see," he said, "that that's why you're here?"

She glanced around the din cave. "In this Godforsaken cave?"

"No, not here in this cave. In Italy," said Michael, "instead of in Paris, with the man you claim to be in love with."

"You don't know me," said Camille, "and you don't know my situation. I'm here because I choose to be. This is my week of freedom, remember, to do with as I see fit. And I don't have to listen to this nonsense if I don't want to."

"No, you don't have to listen," he said, "but you have to face it, sooner or later. You'll see."

"You don't know anything about me."

"I know that you're hiding," said Michael, "and that, deep down, you wish you didn't have to. There's something in you that has to break free. You're here, in Italy, to find what that is. I'm telling you. You have something to declare to the world, and this is where you're going to find what that something is."

"Is that right?" Camille crossed her arms in front of her breasts.

"That's right. It's like when you're at the customs counter at the airport, and the officer will ask, 'Anything to declare?' You'll die a little and answer, 'No', knowing full well that you do. You'll know you want to shout it out from the roof tops, but something in you is keeping you from doing it. You're hiding. But you need to shout it to the world. That way, you can get on with your life and be the person you're supposed to be."

"Hiding something, you say…," said Camille.

"Right, hiding," said Michael. "You need to break free from it and confess what you have inside you."

Camille inhaled slowly. "I have never been able to do the things I wanted to do with my life," she said. "There are so many things, but most of all to be free. Because knowing that I can never do all those things in a week, or even in a lifetime is, well, depressing."

"Oh, come on," said Michael, "don't be like that."

"I have a life I have not chosen," she said. "I have nothing to offer to the world. I have nothing to offer to anyone."

"Oh, come on," he said, "you're just cranky, my pet, you know, because it's so hot in here."

She smiled softly.

He lifted her white binder. "What about these?" he asked. "Your pictures. They're really good. What if you did something with these? You're hiding something here—a true gift and a treasure. Why don't you share it with the world?"

"Sometimes I wish I could."

"There you go."

"So you're an authority on this hiding business, then," she said. The corner of Camille's lip turned up and her eyes widened. She backed away from the flames. "I suppose you have something to declare as well. And that's why you're here, isn't it?"

"I already told you, I'm here to find my half-brother."

"Oh, right, because you're so familial," she said, "I noticed that about you right from the start."

"You could put it that way."

Is he right? she wondered. *Do I really have something to declare? Something great and wonderful to say to the world?* She did not respond to him, but only wondered how he might be right without really knowing anything about her. Keeping it all inside, she merely sighed.

He drank in the soft moan and those pouty lips. *I wish she wouldn't do that. She's so damned cute*, he thought. Allowing her to silently contemplate her situation, he reached into the inside pocket of his leather jacket and pulled out an old monochrome photo of a handsome, young man in an army uniform. Not yet out of his teens, this young gent sported a proud, Roman nose and incredibly thick, black hair that had been greased up and parted in the middle. Michael gently fingered the edges of the photo.

Camille peeked over his shoulder and asked, "Is that your half-brother?"

Michael shook his head with a small grin. He continued to stroke the edges. "I don't have any pictures of my half-brother."

She shrugged.

"This man is a different man. He's nineteen here," said Michael. "Here, take a closer look."

Camille held the photo near the orange flames and studied the young man's features. His eyes bore down on the camera's lens with a solemn stare and his ears jutted out from the wavy, jet black hair. She glanced up at Michael and back to the photo. "Your father?"

Michael nodded and answered, "Bingo."

"I guess you were pretty close to him."

He shook his head. "No, not really."

"Then why are you so determined to find your half-brother?"

"I don't know," said Michael. He answered without thinking, letting his gut do the talking. When he did think about it a moment later, he still could not come up with the reason. "You're the first person to ask me that."

"Maybe you've got something to declare then, too."

"Maybe," he said, then realized her admission. "Hey, wait a minute. You said 'too'. That means you *do* have something to declare."

"I don't really know what it is yet," she said. "You put that thought into my head, my darling. And now we're just going to have to see what happens with it."

They nodded to each other. And for the next few minutes, there was nothing else to say. The only sounds that could be heard inside the cave were the crackling of crumbled twigs and the two travelers' soft steady breaths.

Two hours later, the rain was still coming down very hard.

"I'm tired," said Camille. "And hungry."

"We could catch some spiders and cook them up in the fire," said Michael.

"I think I'll pass," answered Camille. She sent him a sardonic smirk.

Michael scanned the small cave, checking the entrance and the circular walls. "Maybe I can find a snake. I hear they're much tastier than spider." He grinned and wiggled his eyebrows.

Her eyes lit up with worry. "You don't really think there are," she gulped, "snakes?"

"Nah. But I bet they'd be tastier than spiders," he said. He slid his hand into the front pocket of his leather jacket, pulled out a peanut butter candy bar and dangled it out in front of her like a rider dangles a carrot in front of his horse.

Her eyes lit up. "Where did you get that?"

Waving the candy bar around, he said, "You don't really want this good-for-nothing candy bar, do you?" Then he sniffed the wrapper.

Camille licked her lips and he snickered at her.

"You're cruel, you know that?" she said.

He chuckled, and then tossed the bar in the air. It fell in the center of her lap. She tore open the bar greedily and started gnawing on its crunchy, chocolaty, peanut buttery goodness like she hadn't eaten in a week. He grinned at the not-very-lady-like side of her, and was comforted to learn she was real after all.

"Where did you get it?" she said, while chewing on a mouthful.

"I'm the candy man." He winked and made a clicking sound with the inside of his cheeks. Camille giggled and Michael realized he hadn't heard that cackling laugh of hers since the storm had begun. It was only then that he realized, for the very first time, he had missed it. Camille's laugh irritated him like mad, but there was something else about it that he could not put his finger on. All he knew was that he had missed it, like when a striking autumn sunset tucks itself away in behind the hills somewhere. Its forgotten and missed only after seeing it the following autumn.

Michael watched her devour the candy bar as little chocolate semi-circles formed on both sides of her mouth. She transformed into a five-year-old girl in front of him, and he secretly ate up her cuteness. "That's why you have to be prepared. Like the Boy Scouts," Michael said. He reached into his other pocket and pulled out another candy bar, a caramel one. He tore open the package.

"Where do you keep getting all this food from?" asked Camille. "You're like a magician." Her eyes bulged again, begging for more.

"I told you, I'm the candy man," he said, and he bit down on the chewy bar. "I'll keep us alive. Don't you worry about that, my sweet." He wiggled his eyebrows.

Camille finished her peanut butter bar and wiped around her mouth with the back of her hand. "That was really good. Thank you," she said.

"You're welcome." He nodded once, slowly, like a subject bowing to his queen after being rewarded for his valor.

"You know, my sweet," said Camille, "you're not all that bad." She continued to rub at the chocolate around her mouth.

"You admit it?"

"Now don't go and get any crazy ideas, all right?" she said. "I'm an engaged woman." She pointed a finger at him, yawned, and brought her hand to her mouth.

Michael held up his hands in a gesture of surrender and backed away wearing an expression of feigned innocence. Camille stood from her stone, leaned over him and planted a light kiss on his cheek. Then she returned to her stone seat.

An impulse kiss, she thought at first. But honestly, she couldn't explain the reason why she did it, not even to herself. And as for Michael, he didn't know what to think about this kiss that came out of nowhere. He wanted to pursue the matter and see where a peck could lead. He studied her chocolaty-cute, alabaster face, and thought about her cackling laugh and sweet scent. He couldn't get past how provocative she looked in his shirt while her bare feet were propped up on that small rock, her frilly skirt falling loosely over her long, lean legs. *God, she's sexy*, he thought. But then he remembered her warning. He fingered the cold metal lighter and flicked the igniter, but nothing happened.

"I thought you didn't smoke," said Camille.

"I don't." He shook his head, tried the lighter again, but it still did not ignite.

"What's the matter? Broken?" she said.

"Right," he said. "Damned thing is worthless now." And gritting his teeth, he tossed it to the ground.

"It's just a lighter. What's the big deal?"

"Right, just a lighter," he said solemnly.

He stood and ambled over to the cave's entrance to check on the weather. The storm wasn't letting up, and Camille's yawning was now making him sleepy, too. He turned back and said, "Still coming down hard." He threw a few more twigs on the fire and sat back down on his rock. He glanced over at a much calmer Camille.

"Can I ask you a question?" said Camille.

"Shoot."

"I was wondering, is there a grown-up Kim Kruger?" she said.

"I'd really rather not," he started to say, but finished with, "No." He shook his head.

Camille did not know herself why she wanted to know about his love life.

He peered over at her, still thinking about how cute she looked sitting there on her rock. Then he stood, turned away, and faced the dark curved wall. After a long silence, with his back facing her, he began to relate to Camille his life with his ex-wife.

Michael spoke about how he had met Julia ten years earlier, in 1967, at a jazz club in Manhattan. They had fallen for each other right away, and in three months, they were married. Less than a year later, their daughter Angela was born. The excitement was overwhelming for the Valentino family. Michael adored Angela and had cherished his new family with all his heart. He had never been happier. But after Angela's tragic drowning in Coney Island, Michael snapped. No matter how hard he had tried, he could not pull himself out of his wretched misery. Julia had told Michael that she had had enough of his depression, and that she could not forgive him for blaming her for the girl's death. It was an accident, and he could never accept it. It was all she could bear. She left him, but he had never wanted to believe it. He couldn't face it. He had tried to keep the marriage together, but in the end, he had to let Julia go. He had no other choice. It had left Michael with a gaping wound that badly needed healing.

Michael's only child had been taken from him when the girl was just eight years old. "I never even had the chance to say goodbye to her. I just couldn't find the words." Michael paused for a long, deep sigh. "A month after that, Julia was gone, too." He told Camille how not being there to save his drowning daughter ate away at him day and night. He constantly worried whether he would ever be able to have another child. He tried not to let his voice crack, or his eyes well up. He tried not to infect Camille with the sorrow or pain he carried around with him every single day of his wretched life.

Michael paused again. And as he exhaled, he felt Camille's smooth hands slide from behind him and up around his chest. He covered her hands with his own and then turned to face her. She rested a comforting hand on his forearm and gazed up into his dark brown eyes, reached around to the back of his neck, and pulled his head towards hers. A real kiss ensued. It was short, but steady, and passionate. Neither one tried to analyze it; they just let it happen. Camille pulled away first, realizing that as much as she had wanted to, she could not allow this encounter to go any further. Her female intuition told her Michael wanted the same, for their passion to blossom and then explode. "I'm so very sorry," said Camille, her eyes loaded with pain.

With an empathetic smile, Michael shook his head. It was okay that she had kissed him. Whether it was out of sympathy, or pity, or sheer wantonness, it was okay. He wanted her to know that. He wanted her to know that it was a strong kiss—that it had meaning and purpose. He noticed the smudge of chocolate still near her lips, chuckled, and raised a finger to wipe it away. "We'd better get some rest," he said. He exhaled loudly and turned away to gather some dry leaves. He balled them up for a pillow. Then he curled up on the damp ground near the fire.

Camille watched him in his rolled up trousers and candy-making leather jacket, but she didn't move. The kiss had had meaning for her too, and she longed to tell him. But how? She had never been in this sort of situation before, and she didn't know what to do. Everything was upside down, her routine shot to hell, and this man who was not much more than a stranger had poured out his soul to her. More than anything, she wanted a hot shower and a comfortable, king-sized bed in a posh hotel. She didn't want this dank cave with its measly, little fire and chocolate candy bars for dinner. But somehow, that didn't matter how upsetting this place was. "Remember those snakes?" she said, suddenly remembering his joke. "You don't think they're here, right?"

He remained with his back to her, and answered, "Can never be sure."

She gulped, loud enough to be heard in the silent cave, and he smiled with his back still to her. Camille rose up on her bare feet, tip-toed over to him, and very slowly knelt on the ground. Holding her hands up in prayer, finger tips against her lips, the distraught girl was unable to fathom her predicament. She closed her eyes, lay down behind him and reached over his midsection. Her soft touch surprised and aroused him. Then reliving the kiss from moments before, he relaxed. He smiled to himself and closed his eyes, surrendering to unanalyzed acceptance of his situation. The two of them drifted off together in that curled up position as the fire dwindled and then finally died out.

Chapter Fourteen

THE NEXT MORNING ARRIVED WITH A DEWY sunrise. Camille woke just as the sun's rays peeked over the threshold of the small cave. She was wrapped in Michael's jacket, but he was gone. Though alone, she wasn't scared. In fact, she felt more than good. *I did it. I made it through the entire night*, she thought. She smiled and then brought the leather up to her face, closed her eyes, and inhaled a long whiff of his manly scent. *I'd better stop.*

She stood, rubbed the sleep from her eyes, pinched and patted both cheeks with her hands, and smoothed the strands of her long dark hair. She trotted over to the entrance to make sure he wasn't nearby. Then with her back to the world outside, Camille removed his shirt and slipped her dried blouse over her head. Scanning the interior of the cave, a thought popped into her head. She darted over to her small case and pulled out her Nikon and started shooting. It was a dark cave, even in morning. But she thought, *If I can make something out of this creepy place with my pictures, I can make anything work.* To anyone else, the scene may have looked rather odd, for it seemed as if she was shooting at nothing—just unmarked, dark walls and the remnants of a small fire from the night before. But from behind her lens, she saw what a photographer could see before anyone else. She saw the light after the darkness, the calm after the storm. And her imagination was enough to put the images on film.

After she'd been shooting for awhile, Camille packed her camera and photo binder away and was ready to say goodbye to the cave. She picked up Michael's shirt and leather jacket, and took one last look around. With a fresh new feeling of confidence, she lifted her camera case and slung it over her shoulder. Finally, she unfastened one button near the top of her blouse, grinning devilishly to herself on her way out.

Overnight, the storm had blown away the intense heat and now it was just normally hot for Italy's standards. Michael was already outside the cave working on the Fiat. Camille caught a glimpse of his denim-clad legs and backside, while the rest of him was bent over and hidden under the propped hood. With the rustling of fallen leaves, she approached and flung his jacket over her shoulders. "Good morning," he said, raising his head and bare torso.

"Good morning," she called back, chuckling at his appearance. Dried mud had collected in the creases of his pants, and his hands and face were covered in automobile grime. She stifled her laugh and asked, "How's it going?"

"Oh, fine," he said, sticking his nose back inside the little car's engine. "I'm very mechanical, don't you worry, my damsel in distress. We'll be on our way in no time."

She moved next to him and peered down into the engine. "I have no idea what I'm looking at, my pet. Is it bad?" she said.

"No, no, it's fine. Come on. Let's get in," he said, closing the hood. "Just be careful of the top." Sore about last night's attacking branches and the ceaseless rain, the black vinyl roof now seemed to have a mind of its own. It would not yield when Michael tried to unlatch it.

Camille tossed him his tan shirt and he slipped his grease-stained hands through the sleeves.

They propped up the tattered roof, hopped in, and he turned the key. But there was no sound at all. Then on the second try, a short sputtering gave them a glimmer of hope. But then it was silent again. Michael leaped over the little door and flipped up the hood. Camille sat there, blowing a loud raspberry. She leaned over into the rear seat to inspect their luggage, and to her amazement, everything was dry and undamaged. The young woman pulled an emery board from her purse. The unyielding black roof with the hole in the center made the heat unbearable for Camille. So she got out, leaned against the rear quarter panel, and began filing her nails.

"Sure. This'll take no time at all," he said, from behind the raised hood. "I'll have us back on the road in a jiffy." There were a great deal of clanking noises now, as he banged, pulled, and jimmied all sorts of strange-looking parts. The truth was he couldn't tell a spark plug from a radiator hose.

"No rush. Take your time," she said, as she filed away. "Got all day." It was true that Camille had nowhere special that she had to be. Even though technically, this really was her "week of freedom", as she had declared. She would follow where the path would lead; or at least, she had decided that long before she had met Michael.

A quarter of an hour passed. Camille had finished with her nails and now stood at the edge of the road fanning herself with her skirt. And to her surprise, as much as to his, she heard the engine turn over. "I did it!" said Michael, over the noise of the little motor. "Come on, let's go!"

She allowed her skirt to fall back in place and scurried into her seat. Her landing caused the torn roof to come unhinged and bounce up and down, nearly hitting them both on the tops of their heads. Michael shifted into first gear and the Fiat jerked away from the muddy ditch, its tiny wheels skidding onto the black pavement. After the bizarre night that neither of them wanted to talk about, they finally resumed their journey to Rome.

A hundred yards down the road, with a proud feeling of accomplishment, Michael glanced at her. He looked ahead and then stared at her again, and he shot out a loud snort from his nostrils.

"What's so funny?" she said.

"You."

"What?"

"Yeah, you," he said, with a nod and a cackle.

She primped the back of her hair and said, "Darling, what is that supposed to mean?" She fussed with the hair on the other side of her head. "You know, that's not very nice, laughing at a person like that," she said. "Sometimes you can be so——." She pulled down the small sun visor on her side and gazed on her reflection in the tiny mirror. Her face was covered with patches of dried mud and chocolate still surrounded the right side of her mouth. Her usually silken hair looked as frizzy as a doll's after a child had played with it for a very long time. "Aaahhh! Why didn't you tell me?" She wacked him across the upper arm with an open palm.

"I just did," he said, "and you were just about to call me rude or nasty." He chortled at her again.

She smacked him again. He screamed a pretend "Ouch!" and stifled another laugh that sparked a chuckle from Camille. She tried to keep her composure, but the full force of her dizzying laugh exploded. Quite unexpectedly, the laugh wrapped itself around Michael's heart. He reached over at her left cheek and tenderly stroked at a patch of dried mud. A sudden jump in the beat of her heart surprised Camille. She brushed at her own neck, unable to stop the accelerated thumping of her heart. Hoping he had missed it, even though she was sure that he hadn't, she pointed at his face and said, "What about you? I may look a little muddy, but you, my sweet, positively ghastly." She buried her exhilaration with a forced burst of laughter.

Michael craned his neck for a quick glance of himself in the rear view mirror, and it was enough to send a shower of saliva at the glass. After a second look, he said, "You've got to be kidding me." His face was way muddier than hers, like an olive-colored canvas on which various hues of dirty browns were speckled. Swipes of automobile grease and leaf and twig residue accented the work, and his short-cropped hair its tiny clumps of saturated grease was the decorative frame.

Their outburst of hilarity continued until Camille said, "Wait! Stop!"

"What?" Michael eased off the accelerator and turned to face her, worried he had hit something. "What is it?"

"You passed it. Go back."

"Passed what?"

"The exit for Rome. I just saw it. Turn around."

"Are you sure?" he said, swerving and skidding onto the road going in the opposite direction. Immediately up ahead he spotted a small green sign with a white exit arrow that read ROMA.

He exited and the road veered west. "But we've only been driving for five minutes," he said.

Camille turned slowly to glare at the side of his face. "You mean to tell me that I was trapped with you in that smelly, wet cave all night when the city was only five minutes away? How could you!"

"How the hell would I know it was that close?"

They yelled and blamed each other, neither hearing a word of what the other was saying. Then Michael raised an arm and said, "Will you please pipe down so I can try and find the right road?"

"We're on it now, thanks to me," said Camille. "You can't do anything right." She sat with her arms crossed over her chest while shaking her head.

Soon, they were buzzing through the center of Rome. The boisterous streets were like night and day from the country roads they had just passed by. All kinds of vehicles surrounded their Fiat, whizzing by in a frenzied hurry. Camille slammed her eyelids shut and sat with her arms wrapped around her legs. She pressed her feet up against the dashboard, hoping her life wasn't going to end this way. Michael swerved out of the way of a speeding, white Alfa Romeo, just in time to avoid a head-on collision, and Camille shrieked.

"I thought you had your eyes closed," he shouted over the noise.

"One eye! Only one eye!" she yelled back. "If I'm going to die, I thought I'd better watch it happen." A sudden sharp turn flung her from her seat. She landed with her backside on the stick shift. "Ouch!" She whacked his shoulder with an open hand. "Looks like I should make my peace with God!" Her voice was shaky, intense fear was traveling up and down her spine.

Michael nudged the fleshiness of her backside as he reached for the gear shift. "Hey! Watch it!" She swatted his hand and slid her buttocks off the rounded head of the rod and back to her seat.

"Do you mind?" he said, with a devilish smirk. "I'm trying to drive here."

"Yeah, I see what you're trying to do," she said, closely guarding her derrière. "I see exactly what you're trying to do."

Chapter Fifteen

A YOUNG MAN SCURRIED AROUND ONE OF the hotel's thick, marble columns. He was in his early thirties and very handsome—an alluring Don Juan type—with a ruddy complexion and a three-day stubble on his chin. His wavy locks were the color of pitch, and they fell to just above his shoulders. He wore his black vest loosely, and the sleeves on his white button down were rolled up to his elbows. "*Buongiorno*," he said, his face all smiles.

"I have a reservation," said Michael. "I called the day before yesterday."

"Your name, *signore?*" said the dark man.

Michael said, "Michael Valentino."

A female employee rounded the same column and joined the man behind the counter. She was about twenty-two and average height, a knockout with red hair who wore sultry eyes with confidence and class. The man smiled warmly at her. *"Ah. Cecilia, mia cara,"* he said.

Then an attractive, middle-aged woman in a lavender dress passed the front desk. She cocked her head toward the young man behind the counter and he followed her with greedy eyes as she sauntered by. She disappeared through the front door, and the young man turned his attention back to Michael. He said, *"Buongiorno. Prego, signore."*

"A reservation," said Michael. "I called, from Naples."

"Your name?"

"I just told you, Michael Valentino."

"Ah, yes, Signor Valentino," said the man. He glanced down at the counter for clarification of the name. Then he looked up and his eyes went wide. The man quickly looked away, deliberately avoiding Michael's stare.

The dark man's eyes returned to normal. His tone was calm. "But your reservation was for yesterday," he said.

"Yes, I know," said Michael. "I'm sorry, but we had car trouble."

The young man shifted his attention now to Camille. "Ah, together?" he said.

"Well, yes," said Michael. "But uh, no, not really."

"One room or two?" said the man.

"Two."

"Sorry. Only one room left," he said. "Summer time."

"Then why did you ask if we wanted one or two?"

"I was being polite," said the man. "But we can accommodate if it be necessary."

"It be necessary," said Michael.

"Definitely," said Camille.

The redhead Cecilia gazed at Camille. She threw her hand between her colleague and Michael. "Oh, no, no," she said. She looked at the young man. "You were right before. There is only one room left. I checked early this morning."

"Oh?" said the man.

"Yes," said Cecilia. She faced Michael and Camille. "Summer time is *so* busy. You must stay in the one room. I am afraid that is the way it has to be."

"Well, if we have to," said Camille.

Michael sighed. He handed the man his passport.

"You are American," said the man, looking down at the passport.

"From New York," said Michael. "You speak English well."

The young man offered his hand. "My name is Fabio Vitale. I studied the English in university."

"Michael," he said, extending a hand, which the dark man heartily accepted.

"Are you studying, too?" asked Fabio. "Maybe Italian?"

"I'm looking for my half-brother," he said. "And as for my Italian, well, it's not as good as I'd like."

"I can help you with that," he said, all smiles again.

Michael held up his hands in protest. "No, I can't really afford Italian lessons. I'm just here to find my half-brother."

"No, no, no," said Fabio, laughing to himself. "You don't understand. I am always looking to talk to English or American friends, so I can practice. We could help each other."

Camille squealed a girl's giggle and tapped Michael on the shoulder. "That sounds like a grand idea, my darling," she said. "One can always use more friends."

Cecilia smiled at her. "*Si.* It is most important to have friends," she said.

Michael nodded. "You're right, my pet," he said. "I like the idea." He held out his hand one more time. "You've got a deal, Mr…what was it?"

"Fabio," said the young man, proudly slapping himself on his chest with his free hand. "Call me Fabio."

"All right. And you can call me Michael," said Michael.

"Michele," he said. "I will call you Michele."

"Michele it is, then," said Michael, shrugging.

"Deal." Fabio shook his hand with vigor.

"Fabio!" The shout came from a man emerging from a back office. He was a bald, stocky man in his fifties who was wearing a starched white shirt, a black suit, and a serious expression. Drenched with perspiration, he came towards them with his hands waving frantically.

Fabio winced. "That is the *capo*, my boss," he said, with one side of his mouth cupped. "He thinks he is the owner."

Fabio ignored his boss, and continued with the new guests. "I will check you in. You go to your room. I will finish work soon, and then we can talk, if you are not being busy."

Michael shook his head. "No, I'm not that busy," he said, looking down at the watch on his wrist. He faced Camille. "What about you, my sweet?"

She lowered her eyelids and shook her head. "The bath tub awaits me," she said. "And I suggest you make a visit of your own very soon."

"I'm a shower guy," said Michael. He glanced at Fabio and said, "I'm surprised you didn't say anything about our appearance."

"I am used to it," said Fabio. "We get many types here."

"Yes, many types," said Cecilia.

"I like you, Fabio," said Michael. He shook his hand again. "I like you."

Fabio smiled at him and said, "You go to the room for the shower. I wait for you here." He handed Michael the key to Room 207.

Michael and Camille left the front desk and headed to their room. Fabio turned to Cecilia and said, "Did we do the right thing?"

"*Si.* There was no other way," said Cecilia. "You saw their faces, no?"

"Yes, I saw," said Fabio.

"I saw too," said Cecilia. "And now we must find a way to finish it."

"*Si.* I go with him and you go with her," said Fabio. "To make sure they are. Then we finish it."

Cecilia nodded. "*Si.*"

Twenty minutes later, Michael thumped down the marble stairs to the lobby. Fabio was in front of the desk, talking with Cecilia, who stood behind the counter. Fabio tapped her lightly on the cheek and approached Michael. Michael wondered about this dashing young man. What kind of a person was he? What did it mean, to "help each other"? He had never in his life come to an agreement like that so quickly. But he decided to go with his gut and didn't worry about it. Fabio grabbed Michael by the wrist and started to move away from the front desk. When Fabio noticed his boss hurrying towards him, he shouted a goodbye. But the sweaty, bald man called out, "Eh, Fabio! You miss those two guests over there." He pointed to a young couple who had just entered the lobby with their large baggage in tow.

"I don't see any guests, *Capo*," said Fabio. He turned back to the young woman behind the front desk. "Maybe Cecilia sees them," he said to the boss. Then turned to her, and added, "Eh, Cecilia?" He flung his black sports jacket over one shoulder and tugged on Michael's arm.

"Get the haircut, eh?" said the boss. Watching the young man dash away, the boss realized that this adventurous boy was already done working for the day, no matter what he would have said. And he wouldn't get a haircut.

Fabio turned back and smirked at him. "You just jealous, *Capo*." He turned again and, with four fingers, flipped the black curls at the base of his neck. "Have to go, *Capo*. The night, she is young. And so I am." Then he tugged on Michael's shirt sleeve again. "Let's go, Michele."

The boss stood with his arms folded, shaking his head. "Always in a hurry, that boy," he said to himself. "Always in a hurry."

"Let's go," said Fabio, as he and Michael made it through the revolving door. "I buy you lunch. Do you have a car?"

"Yeah, but it's badly damaged," said Michael. "It's right over there." He pointed to the beat-up Fiat.

"No good," said Fabio. "We walk."

"But why don't we eat at the hotel?" said Michael, chasing after the young man.

"I want to talk English, in the open."

"Ok," said Michael. He pulled a piece of paper from his pocket and looked down at it. "Fabio, do you know this place? Via dei Cappellari?"

Fabio looked at the paper. "Via die Cappellari. *Si, Certo,*" he said. "I will take you there."

"Great."

"But first, we have lunch."

They walked along a fairly straight, narrow stretch of pavement until they were standing in front of a tiny panini shop that had three grilled sandwiches on display in its small front window next to the door. Fabio pushed open the glass door and Michael followed him inside. The shop was nothing more than a short, high counter with twenty or so different types of Italian sandwiches behind glass and ready to go. There was an old, brass cash register and a small refrigerator filled with water, juice, soda, and beer.

Behind the counter was just one attendant, the owner, who took care of everything. Fabio turned to Michael and said, "Which one do you like?"

"I think I like that one," said Michael, "with the prosciutto, eggplant and sun-dried tomatoes."

"Good choice, Michele."

Fabio ordered it for Michael along with his own salami and olive sandwich, then paid the man and handed Michael his lunch. Outside the small shop, he led Michael to a square down at the end of the shop-lined street, where the two men found an empty stone bench. Under the shade of an arching hazelnut tree, Fabio gestured for Michael to begin eating.

Michael bit down and a celebration of flavors swirled around the inside of his mouth. He nodded his approval as he chewed.

Fabio also took a bite, and after swallowing, he said, "So, Michele, tell me, why you are here, in my little town of Roma, all the way from New York?"

Michael said, "I'm looking for my half-brother." Then he spoke of how his search had begun in a little corner of Naples, and how his only lead brought him to Rome. Michael found himself opening up to the swarthy Fabio. The words poured forth from him like the rushing rapids through a ruptured dyke. He admitted that he might have been running away from his life in New York, or perhaps been looking for a new one. He spoke of his hope to connect with his half-brother and share the rest of their lives together as true brothers, stressing how very important it was that he did not fail in his quest. Staring deep into the other man's eyes, he said, "Fabio, my family is shrinking. And this may be our last hope to hold it together."

Fabio peered back at the desperate man. "You overreact, Michele," he said. "You are too emotional. Don't worry. You will find him."

On more than one occasion, Fabio had been accused of being an overly passionate fellow. He had known Michael a mere two hours, and he could already feel the strength and sincerity of his desire to contact his half-brother. Fabio already knew how much this meant to Michael, and needed little convincing of his tenacity.

The two new friends chewed away on their sandwiches and washed them down with some crisp sparkling water. They talked and laughed, about family and food, women and love. And under that shady hazelnut tree on their stone bench, they formed a bond that would last the rest of their lives.

Chapter Sixteen

"WHAT ARE YOU DOING?" SAID THE TALL, blonde woman to the shorter Cecilia behind the front desk counter. "Signor Stanza will see you. Stand up straight."

"I cannot," said Cecilia. "It is just so boring, Patrizia. And it is too hot. I cannot take it anymore." She fanned herself with a notepad, her swaying breasts concealed in a neck-hugging maroon top.

"Come on," said Patrizia. "You said you were going to behave today." She nudged her co-worker with her elbow.

"*Si*, and you said you were going to go out with me for a drink," said Cecilia. "Two weeks ago." She eyed Patrizia. "And I am still waiting." She stood up straight and crossed her arms, pushing the sleeves of the maroon blouse halfway up her arms.

"I cannot," said Patrizia. "I have a date. With Marco."

"Hooray!" said Cecilia. "It's about time."

"Yes, and I am leaving work now," said Patrizia, "to get ready. You will have to take care of the rest of the guests." She gestured with a nod to the one now approaching. It was Camille.

"All right, all right," said Cecilia, pushing Patrizia away at her hips, "*vai, vai.* Go already."

Patrizia smiled at Camille, patted Cecilia's arm gently, and dashed away from the lobby. Cecilia acknowledged Camille and said, "Have you ever noticed? There are no men in this hotel, only women. Don't you find that odd?"

"Well, I," said Camille, in a stammer, "I think there must be at least one man."

"Oh, you think?"

"Why sure. I'm staying with a man in my room."

"Of course you are," said Cecilia, "and he is tall and gorgeous with nice muscles and a manly jaw."

"I don't think you could say any of those things about him," said Camille. "To tell the truth, I really don't know him all that much."

"You are modest," said Cecilia. "Because he is your man and you do not want me to steal him away."

"Oh, no," said Camille. "He is not my man, I assure you. My man is in Paris."

"Then I can steal your roommate?"

"Be my guest," said Camille.

Cecilia noticed the flushing of Camille's cheeks and said, "You are sure?"

Camille threw her hands up and said, "Have at him. We're only staying in the same room together because we have to. You told us that there was only one room left because of the summer season. Remember?"

"Yes, yes. There was only one room left in this hotel," said Cecilia. She looked away.

"It was the truth, wasn't it?"

Cecilia smiled and said, "*Certo*. Of course."

Camille looked Cecilia up and down. "Do you really mean to go after Michael?"

"Who is Michael?"

"The man in my room."

"Oh, yes."

Cecilia rounded the front desk, locked arms with Camille, and as she guided her through the lobby, said, "Come on, we find out everything about your Michael now."

"But what about your boyfriend?" asked Camille. She checked out Cecilia's impressive figure and sultry smile. "I assume you have a boyfriend."

"Of course," she said. "I have two."

Cecilia looked at Camille as if this was perfectly understandable and acceptable. And Camille said, "Well then, what about your job? Don't you have to work?" She turned back to the front desk.

"I leave that to Signor Stanza."

"But isn't he your boss?"

Cecilia grinned and said, "*Essatamente*."

The two young women whirled through the revolving front door. Outside in the summer sunshine, Camille gently tugged back on Cecilia's arms.

Cecilia stopped and said, "What is your name?"

"Camille."

"I am Cecilia."

Camille smiled at her, and Cecilia smiled back. She said, "Cecilia?"

"*Sì?*"

"Then you're not serious about your boyfriend?"

"Maurizio?" said Cecilia. Her eyelids lowered halfway down as she breathed in deeply, imagining the manly scent of him. "Yum."

"Okay, Maurizio." Camille nodded.

"Of course I am serious," said Cecilia. "But I am also serious about Vittorio. When I am with Vittorio, the passion we share is just like magic. And it is the same with Maurizio."

"Cecilia, I don't understand," said Camille, shaking her head.

"What is it?"

"How can you have the same passion for two men, at the same time?" she said, wondering if she was crossing some cultural boundary.

But Cecilia did not flinch. "You see, Camille," she said, "men, they are really boys, especially Italian men. They act grown up, sophisticated, strong, and smart. But really, they are just boys. And boys, they like to play. Even play with us, like we are their toys. That is why, as a woman, you must always be in control, and never let them play with you. *You* play with them. You must treat men like they think they can treat us, *capisce*?"

"I'm not sure," said Camille.

"You must learn when to act, when to take charge, when to trust," said Cecilia. "And to make it look like they are in charge the whole time." Then she raised an index finger. "A man is like a dog. He can be trained to bring you slippers or to do tricks for you. And he learns who is master. But if you keep him tied up in a small cage, he will want to run free in the open field to chase all kinds of animals. Give him space to run and play, and he will soon become tired. He will always come back to you. That is the only way you can train a man." She pointed her finger at Camille. "Make him think he is in charge."

"Now I think I understand what you're saying," said Camille. "I just don't know. I'm not like you." Camille wanted to believe that true love was different than the casual affair. That it was open and honest and pure, and it was the only way a relationship was ever going to succeed.

"Come, we go," said Cecilia. "It is time to find out everything."

They walked lazily down a quiet lane, one that looked as if all the Roman residents had abandoned. Camille wondered how it was possible in this city that seemed to her to be always full of life. But it lasted no more than a few minutes. Then they arrived at the planned destination.

Cecilia gazed up at the awning of the café. She read the small sign just below. "It's about time," she said.

Camille stared at her and said, "What do you mean?"

"For more than two weeks, and Patrizia never go out drinking with me. I think she have too many boyfriends."

"Well, I'm here with you now," said Camille.

"That's right," said Cecilia, "and we are going to find out everything."

The two girls entered Bar Tarantola, a claustrophobic bar located in a three-story, brick building sandwiched between a leather goods shop and a nail salon. Each of the six tiny tables was occupied, and there were only three empty stools left at the bar.

"I like to drink, Cecilia," said Camille. "Especially wine." The images flooded back instantly. The Chianti at Montesole Castle that had made she and Michael tipsy in the garden… A sad regret hit her hard. *What if I had taken things between us a little further?* She drove the thought quickly from her mind.

Cecilia indicated the empty bar stools and the girls sat. The bartender approached, drying a tumbler with a plain, white bar towel. He was about twenty-five, dark, and very handsome. He saw that the girls were talking and waited for a pause.

Cecilia looked up from her stool and gazed on his chiseled features. She smiled and he said, "*Prego.*"

She answered him with English. "We will have," Cecilia paused, looked over at Camille and asked, "Something that's not wine, it's okay?"

When Camille nodded, Cecilia faced the bartender again and said, "Amaretto."

He turned and grabbed the bottle from a glass shelf behind him and poured the almond liqueur over ice in two old tumblers and set them in front of the girls. Cecilia smiled again at him, and the sexy stranger winked back.

Camille caught Cecilia's eye and waited for him to walk away before asking, "Cecilia, how can you do that?"

"Do what?" Feigning ignorance, a sly smirk formed on her lips.

Camille smiled playfully now and said, "You know." She gestured with a sideways nod at the swarthy man. "You have Maurizio *and* Vittorio."

"Oh, Camille, that was nothing. Just playing."

"Do you always play like that when you go to bars?"

"Not only bars," said Cecilia. Her eyelids fell slowly as she caught the bartender's stare. She batted her lashes and then looked back at Camille.

Camille chuckled softly and said, "You're something else, Cecilia."

She grinned and said, "I know. *Grazie.*"

The girls toasted their health and swallowed, savoring the bittersweet almond flavor. Cecilia looked around the shadowy room for a table that might have been vacated, but there was still none. She peered at the faces, the two couples sitting together slowly sipping red wine, the group of four young men on the make who would undoubtedly forget their one-night lovers the next morning, and the loners occupying the other black stools at the bar. "Look at them, Camille," she said.

"Who?"

"All of them." Cecilia gestured with a small wave. "Do you see any you like?"

"Cecilia!" Camille whispered it, but said it with a scolding tone.

"Do not be shy," said Cecilia. She swept a hand over the room. "This is *Italia*, we are all lovers. Everybody knows."

"You mean...?"

"*Si*. We come to the bar to look. But not only the bar. We go to the café, trattoria, market, anywhere. We always look. It is natural."

A protesting scorn covered Camille's face. "But I am an engaged woman," she said. "I can't be looking like that." She shook her head. "No, not like that."

Cecilia paused a moment. She glanced at the bartender, but he was busy fixing a drink. "Why, you do not think your Claude has eyes for other women?" she said.

"Of course not. Never," said Camille. *How could Cecilia even ask that?* This would never have crossed Camille's mind, since Claude was the perfect gentleman. He always had been, and he always would be.

Sipping her drink, Cecilia tilted her head and lowered one eyelid while staring Camille down. "Never?"

"Never." But after a brief pause, Camille said, "Well, maybe he has looked. But that's all. I trust Claude completely."

"Of course you do," said Cecilia. She hated to think her new friend Camille would believe cheating could not happen to her.

Camille eyed Cecilia suspiciously, hoping she didn't really believe in such a cynical world. No matter what part Camille played on the outside, in her heart she wanted to believe in true love. She had to believe, because she knew she had nothing else. As childhood sweethearts, her mother and father had fallen in love, married and had Camille. They were still happy together after many years. *That's the way it happens in life. That's the way things are.*

"And you, Camille?" said Cecilia.

"Me what?" She swirled the amber liqueur and ice in her glass.

Noticing Camille now with her eyes fixed on the handsome bartender, Cecilia said, "Your eyes, they have never roamed?"

"Cecilia."

"Come on, tell the truth," she said. "We are friends. Do not be shy."

Ever since that fateful night in the cave with Michael, Camille had been dying to tell someone what had happened between them, and now she had the perfect opportunity. She didn't even have to bring it up or excuse or explain herself. She could lay her cards on the table with no tip-toeing around the issue and would no longer have to deny it. Somehow, she knew she could trust her new friend. "Well, there is one man," she said.

"I knew it," said Cecilia. "Tell me, tell me." She waved her fingers in a greedy manner.

Camille hesitated. "He is…"

Cecilia's eyes danced a dance of anticipation. "Yes?"

"Italian."

"Ah-ha. *Santa Maria*," said Cecilia. She reached to the sky with extended fingers.

"Well, not exactly Italian." said Camille.

Cecilia crinkled her brows. "What do you mean 'not exactly'?" she said.

"Well, he's from New York," she said, shrugging her shoulders. "But his family is Italian," she said.

"Michele?" asked Cecilia, "Michele from your room? Ah, nobody's perfect."

Camille immediately waved it away with her hand. "No, never mind. I didn't mean any of it. It's just because I miss Claude." But as she spoke, she thought of Michael, not Claude, and her face lit up and her eyes sparkled. After spending that night in the cave with him, something had been stirred in Camille. It was something that she could not explain, and it opened emotions that she could not control. "Being with him gave me the chance to challenge myself, be a little dangerous, and stretch my limits. He allows me to be a person I never knew I could be."

Cecilia watched Camille's face blush and her voice crack as she spoke about Michael. "*Capito*. I see," she said.

"Oh, no, that's not it," said Camille. "No, no. I'm not in love with him, Cecilia. He's like a brother to me. Or, an old pair of pajamas, you know? Someone comfortable, who you can rely on for help. Like that." She hurried the words out, hoping that if she had said them fast enough, she could believe in them herself.

"Old pajamas," said Cecilia, "they are hard to throw away."

"Oh, no, Cecilia," said Camille, nervously thinking the worst. "I don't even need to tell Claude about Michael. He doesn't have to know, because it's nothing. This other man means nothing to me. You understand, right?"

"Oh, I will not say anything," said Cecilia, inwardly pleased with the feeling that her friend's little secret would work its way to the surface some way.

Camille let an embarrassed chuckle escape. "Just forget it, okay?" she said. "It's just a silly thing."

Cecilia chuckled in return, and then rubbed Camille's arm. "Camille, you are so young," she said, "and pure. You do not see what is in front of your face. He is the one for you, this Michael in your room." Cecilia was only twenty-two, but she was wise in the art of love. She knew how to toy with her man-puppets like a true master. And although she hadn't yet found true love in her warm heart, she knew it when she saw it.

"You're crazy," said Camille. For so long, she had wondered what it would sound like out loud, if someone, even she herself had spoken of the passion she felt brewing in her heart. She felt a constant ache from being apart from Michael for even a few moments. Now that she knew what it felt like, she recognized that it was all too sweet and all too bitter. "No, Cecilia, I could never leave Claude. I have known him too long."

"Darling Camille." Cecilia held Camille's face in her hands and then stroked her cheeks. "Sweet Camille, you are a nice girl. But you are in love. *Amore*. I know, Camille. I know these things," she said, waving an index finger in the air.

"How do you know?"

"I am Italian," she said. "Italians talk with our hands," she demonstrated by extending tanned arms and flailing them about, "and love with our eyes, like this." She seductively lowered her lids and glanced over at the handsome bartender, who winked back. Keeping her eyes glued to him, she said, "Love is the most important thing in the world."

Camille watched Cecilia, who had her eyes still glued on the bartender. "I still say you're crazy," she said.

Cecilia winked back at the bartender, and then finally turned to face Camille. "If you like," she said with a small smile. "But I know. You will go and try to get him, this Michael in your room."

Camille gazed on Cecilia, and said nothing.

"But before that, let's have some fun, ah?" Cecilia raised her head and let her seductive eyes dance around the small stuffy room.

Chapter Seventeen

FABIO THOUGHT HE WOULD BOOST MICHAEL'S mood. After lunch, Fabio had taken Michael to meet the first owner of the cigar shop in Naples who had moved back to Rome. Michael had remembered what the second Signor Bagliore had told him about the flowers. But Signor Bagliore number one no longer lived on Via dei Cappellari. The husband and wife who now owned the house had told Fabio that Signor Bagliore had moved away to America to be with his son and daughter-in-law. They had bought a very nice home in California and Signor Bagliore and his wife had decided to live with them there. Fabio felt terrible about it. He knew Michael was close to giving up on finding his half-brother. He had thrown the flowers in the street and told Fabio it was no use. It was like finding a needle in a haystack. So Fabio would now make it up to his new friend. He left the front desk and climbed the stairs to

Michael's room. He didn't even knock and flung the door open. He found Michael sulking on the bed. Fabio ordered him to wash up and get dressed, explaining that it was no good brooding and feeling down, and that he shouldn't give up. Michael's half-brother was out there somewhere, and with Fabio's help, he would find him. "Come on, Michele, hurry. Tonight, I will show you the real Italia."

A protesting Michael showered, and then threw on a pair of jeans and an old brown T-shirt. But Fabio scolded him. "No, Michele, he said," we are not in America. I am showing you Italy tonight. You must dress the part."

He dragged Michael by the arm and rummaged through his closet, finding a pair of black gabardine trousers and a long-sleeved, white shirt. Fabio tossed the garments on the bed. "This is what you wear tonight. Now change."

Michael slumped onto the bed, while Fabio stood over him with arms folded, making sure he did not renege.

They left Michael's room and crept down the stairs and through the lobby. Signor Stanza caught them sneaking off, but they were already winding through the revolving door before he could shout anything.

Fabio's shiny, black motorcycle was parked in front of the hotel. Michael shook his head. "I'm not going on that thing," he said.

Fabio smirked at him and said, "Oh, yes you are. Hop on, Michele. We have to see *Italia* now. And this is the best way." He jumped on the bike, turned, and patted the black leather seat behind him. Michael sighed loudly, but straddled the seat behind Fabio.

Twenty minutes later, the sleek, black bike was flying past hilly rows of cypress and hazelnut trees that were standing tall on either side of the winding, paved road. The bike raced up and down the hills and the wind was streaming through Fabio's thick black curls. Michael whisked them out of his face a few times. "You know, Michele, you are being grouchy. And you need not to be grouchy no more."

"Is that right?"

"*Si*. Look out there," he said. "Beautiful Italian country-side." He took one hand from the handlebars and gestured to his right. "I think Italian scenery is more gorgeous than scenery in America, eh, Michele?"

"I don't know." Michael ignored the beauty of the land with its comforting sun. Just twenty minutes outside Rome, the countryside was magnificent with its undulating verdant hills and row upon row of lemon, cypress, and hazelnut trees.

"Come on, Michele, look."

Michael figured Fabio was not going to let up, so he turned to view the landscape. "I've seen it," is all he said, re-calling the magnificent views during the drive to Rome with Camille in the beat-up Fiat.

Another twenty minutes went by, and they were back in Rome. Fabio continued on slowly as he weaved through the vehicles and pedestrians, and then finally stopped on Via Roma. He parked in front of a cute café and the two men hopped off the bike. "Good. I missed my coffee this morning," said Michael.

"Oh, you think we should have some *caffè?*"

"Isn't that why I got all dressed up?"

Fabio chuckled as they sat at a table outside. A young waitress with short black bangs sidled up to them and quietly asked to take their order. Fabio asked for two coffees and two small cakes. The shy girl smiled and turned. Fabio watched her walk away, his eyes glued to the curve of her hips, smoothly enhanced by the tight, black skirt into which she had somehow managed to squeeze. "What do you think, Michele?" he said, nudging his nose in the direction of the shapely girl.

Michael hadn't been paying much attention to her. "She's cute. I guess," he said.

Fabio finally released his stare from the girl and turned to Michael. "Michele, what's wrong?" he said. "That *signorina,* she is *molto bella.* And *molto* sexy. And you do not even look?"

"I'm sorry, Fabio," he said. "I'm just tired. And I'm starting to believe I'm never going to find my half-brother. Maybe it was a stupid mistake to come to Italy."

"Michele, how can you say that?" said Fabio. "If you did not come to Italy, how can we become friends, eh?" He slapped him on the back and his hand remained there for a moment.

"You're right, Fabio," said Michael. "I shouldn't have said that."

"That's okay," said Fabio. "We are friends. We forgive."

Michael cracked a smile. Fabio peeked inside the café and spotted the waitress. "Michele, here she comes. This time, you look, *capisce?*"

"Okay, I'll look."

The young girl approached and set their order down on the black metal table. This time, Michael noticed that her very black hair was cut short and curled in toward the back of her neck. Her face was round and her eyes were deep brown and large. Her full dark eyebrows peeked through her straight, silky bangs. The girl's skin was fair and smooth, with rosy cheeks that held a hint of innocence leftover from childhood. Smiling silently, she left the bill on the table and trotted away.

"Okay, *more* than cute," said Michael. "You win."

"That's more like it," said Fabio. "Now you are being *Italiano.*" A huge grin of victory planted itself on his fine-looking face.

"Is this what you do all day, Fabio?" said Michael. "Drink coffee and check out pretty girls? This is being Italian?"

"*Si. Esattamente,*" said Fabio. "It is being *Italiano.* Now you understand, no?" He raised his small, white cup in a toast and waited for Michael to do the same.

Michael tapped his cup to Fabio's, but at the same time, he shrugged his shoulders. *What are we doing?* he thought.

Under the shade of the red and brown awning, the two friends sat for ten more minutes, finishing their coffees and cakes. And of course, watching more pretty girls. Some passed by on the busy street on their way home from work, some were off to a night of shopping or visiting friends. Others stopped in to the café for a drink or small bite to eat. Fabio winked at a few and coaxed Michael to be more friendly with them, but since he was new at being "*Italiano*", Michael only observed, studying the ways of his teacher. Reading Michael's apprehension, Fabio had assured him that what they were doing was completely natural, and quite acceptable.

When the waitress passed by their table, Fabio pressed his hand to her forearm. She stopped and asked if there was anything else they wanted, but Fabio shook his head and told her he had just wanted to see her face one more time. The girl blushed, and smiled timidly. She thanked them graciously and slipped away. Watching her swaying hips, Fabio stood and tossed some money on the table.

"How could you do that, Fabio?" said Michael, standing after his friend. "You've got guts, pal."

"Michele, does that meaning I am being *Italiano*? Guts?"

"Yeah, I guess it does."

They left the café and sauntered a while through the charming town, down the old, narrow streets lined with bright new shops, cafés, and restaurants. Fabio was in no particular hurry. It annoyed Michael as he pondered whether there was any purpose to their little stroll. Why would his friend take him to a shopping and dining area catering to visitors? What was Fabio's motive? It irked Michael, especially Fabio's slow pace of life. The frustration brewed inside him.

But Fabio ignored Michael and gazed at the pedestrians. He spied a retired couple coming out of a jewelry store. They joined the end of a line of tourists waiting to board a chartered bus. He watched as the portly man, loaded down with shopping bags, struggled to check the time on his wristwatch. Unsuccessful, he asked his wife for the time, who checked her watch and then mentioned that they were going to finish shopping the following day, since they needed to be back at the hotel by seven to make their spa appointment. And then dinner was at eight. A long hard sigh emerged from the tired man with the large belly.

The couple boarded the bus. Fabio shook his head and laughed.

"What is it, Fabio?" asked Michael.

Fabio gestured with a head nod to the couple. "Those people that got on that bus. They are funny."

"Why funny?"

"Well, they're in a hurry, to do what?" Fabio said. He knew Michael's frustration from a few moments earlier had also been a waste of energy. Michael was just as guilty as the couple who boarded the bus, and Fabio would not let it go.

"What do you mean?" asked Michael.

"They're hurrying around this place, to buy things they think their friends and family would want," said Fabio. "You know, souvenirs. They're doing other things that really do not make sense. It's like they have to keep to a time schedule. They have a certain amount of hours for this and a certain amount of hours for that."

"And?"

"Well, it does not make any sense," said Fabio. "They're on holiday in my *Italia*, thousands of miles away from home. They probably saved *molto* money for this trip. And once they get here, they struggle with packages and appointments. If this is how they live all the time, when do they ever enjoy their life? They should do things the *Italia* way."

"Hmm." Michael watched the bus pull away. "That sort of makes sense," he said.

"*Si. Il dolce far niente*," said Fabio. "You are understanding, Michele." He slapped Michael on his shoulder. Michael was puzzled still, and just shook his head as they meandered along.

Three blocks later, parched and sweaty, Michael allowed a heavy sigh to escape. Fabio turned to him and said, "Michele, you look tired. We should get the gelato, and take a break."

"Whatever you say."

The men stopped in at a corner gelateria. A glass dome showcased the owner's one hundred-odd flavors. Michael chose hazelnut and Fabio chose pistachio. Outside, they walked no more than fifty yards, and the narrow, tree-lined street opened up to a bright, stone-paved piazza. The ochre ring of the piazza contained a large stone statue in the center. Michael peered up to see a seated Roman god with long curly locks and beard, and a staff at the ready. The god was surrounded by dolphins. Other ancient gods were perched atop their pedestals that circled the piazza's perimeter. Fabio and Michael ambled to one of the stone benches that were draped in shade from a low-hanging hazelnut tree. Michael held his dripping gelato in one hand and rolled up his sleeve with the other. Then he switched hands and rolled up the opposite sleeve. "You made me change out of my jeans for this?" he said. "Dress clothes for gelato? I don't get it."

Lapping up his gelato lovingly, Fabio said, "The clothes are not for the gelato, Michele." He licked at his cone and continued, "They are to make you look good and feel good. When you wear the clothes, you are looking good, stylish, and modern. You are looking *Italiano*. It does not matter what you are doing. What is important is how you are feeling. That is why we say, *il dolce far niente*."

"But what *are* we doing, Fabio?" said Michael. "Here. What are we doing here? In this place?"

"Nothing," said Fabio. "We eat the gelato. And we do nothing."

Michael searched his friend's face. He watched him lick the Italian ice cream, surrounding it with his mouth like he was making love to a gorgeous, Italian lady. Michael's hazelnut gelato dripped over the cone onto his hand, the wet cold snapping him out of his daydream. He caught the dripping gelato with his tongue, while still studying Fabio's manner. "You know something, Fabio?" he said. His friend mumbled, only slightly paying attention. "You're right." Michael thought about home, where everyone in the mad city of New York was always doing something. Everyone was always busy. Busy working, busy shopping and busy commuting. Even on vacation they had to be doing something, like those tourists he had seen getting on that bus. *I'm always doing something, too.* He wondered why every moment in life had to be filled with doing something. During every minute and every second, something had to be happening. Why couldn't people just live without that something happening? The more he thought about it, the more he realized just how sickening it all was. He closed his eyes and rubbed them. When he opened them, he felt something new. Something was different about him. Something had changed in him. Nodding, he continued, "You're right, my friend. I'm tired of running around. And I don't want to be like that anymore."

"Now you are getting it."

"I am?" said Michael. "Yeah, I am. I mean, look at those kids out there." Six adolescents were splashing about in the center stone fountain. "They're having fun getting wet and cooling off. And they don't care what anyone thought or said about them. They have no worries and no stress. Isn't that what life's supposed to be like?"

"For me, it is," said Fabio.

"Maybe for me, too," said Michael. And without realizing it, the gelato had disappeared. Michael looked down at his sticky hand and smiled. Then gazing on the playing children again, he asked Fabio if he wanted children some day. Fabio answered with a resounding yes and then told Michael, as a man, it was his duty to have babies. How else could he ever pass down all that he was?

Michael agreed, and after a pause said, "Fabio, you have many girls. More than one, is this true?"

"*Si*, Michele, I have," he said. "Many more."

"Well, my friend, I don't even have one," he said. "But in my world, one is plenty." Then he took a moment to reflect on his time with Camille. Though it was only a few hours since he had last seen her, he found himself missing her and wanting to see her again. "Do you think I am wrong to feel this way?"

"Maybe I understand you," said Fabio. "You are deep in your heart. I hope I can see this 'one is plenty' girl some day."

A smiling Michael playfully smacked Fabio on his back and reclined on the stone bench. "Me too."

"You are smart, Michele," said Fabio. "But you are maybe only half *Italiano* now. So you need me for teaching you the other half, no?"

"You're the teacher."

"Yes. And tonight you will learn the other half."

"Why? What's tonight?"

"You will see, Michele," said Fabio, his mischievous smirk brightening his dark features. "You will see."

Chapter Eighteen

MICHAEL TURNED THE KEY IN THE DOOR to his hotel room. He walked inside looking at his shoes. Then he checked the clock on the nightstand. It showed six o'clock. He sighed and moved closer to the bathroom. But he heard running water and stopped right before turning the door knob. Fabio burst into the room seconds later. Michael didn't even have a chance to flip off his shoes and rest on the bed for a few minutes.

"You are not ready?" said Fabio.

Michael sighed. "Fabio, I just got here," he said.

"What took you so long?" asked Fabio "I dropped you off two hours ago. Where did you go?"

"Nowhere," said Michael.

"Nowhere?"

"Just around the neighborhood," said Michael. "I took a walk. I didn't want to talk to anyone. I wanted to think."

"What is there to think?" asked Fabio.

Michael looked away from Fabio and said, "I don't know."

"You were brooding?"

"I wasn't brooding."

"Yes, you were," said Fabio.

"I was thinking about how I'm never going to meet my half-brother."

"Michele, haven't you learned anything about what I told you?" asked Fabio. "Do you not believe in my *Italia*? Do you not yet admit that *il dolce far niente* is the best life for you?"

"I don't know," said Michael. "It's too hard to be positive when I feel like this."

"That is enough. Come, you get ready for tonight," said Fabio. "Let us see what is in your closet to wear."

The doorknob on the bathroom door turned. Camille stepped out of the bathroom. She was wearing only a white bath towel. It was tucked in above her chest and reached down to mid thigh.

Both men's heads turned. Michael realized he hadn't seen her since the morning. She was radiant. Michael wondered if she had soaped up with the same soap he was using. He didn't realize how much he had missed her.

While Fabio walked over to her and kissed the back of her hand. A few drops of water fell to his lips. He smiled at her and licked his lips, making sure Michael saw. Then he said, "*Bella*. How beautiful you are right after the shower."

Camille tightened her grasp on the towel. "I didn't expect anyone," she said. She twisted the towel tighter.

Michael pushed Fabio from the back. "Fabio was just leaving," he said.

"No, I wasn't," said Fabio. "I came up to wait for Michele. We are going to dinner at a nice pizzeria. Very close to here. Would you join us?"

"Oh, that's very kind of you," said Camille. "But I'm going to dinner too, with Cecilia."

"How nice," said Fabio. "Pizza?'

"No, Cecilia said something about amatriciana," said Camille.

"I like amatriciana," said Michael.

"Yes, but you have a date with Fabio. Right, Fabio?" Camille grinned.

"You are correct, Camilla," said Fabio. "Although, I would trade him for you any day. And Cecilia, well…"

"Yes, well…" said Camille. "Do you and she…?"

"Oh, no. We are just friends," said Fabio. "I have not yet found my one is plenty girl." He faced Michael. "Did I say it correctly?"

Michael looked away and said, "Yeah. Just perfect."

"Well, I can get ready in the bathroom," said Camille. She walked over to the closet. "Let me just grab my dress."

As she did, the two men watched her move. She swayed and bent in the way only a woman could. She chose a deep blue evening dress and walked back to the bathroom. Before closing the door, she said, "Good night, gentlemen. And have a nice time."

Michael brushed at his chin and said, "Yeah. You too."

Fabio said, "*Arrivederci, bella*. Cecilia is very lucky to have you tonight."

Camille waved goodbye and closed the bathroom door.

Michael nudged Fabio's shoulder. "Come on. Let's go," he said. "I don't want to see her when she comes out. She'll look too damned good."

"You don't want to see?" asked Fabio. He shook his head and clicked his tongue. "You are still not *Italiano*, Michele. I want to see, and I am not even in love. You need another lesson."

They left the room and Camille peeked her head out from the bathroom. She nodded and said, "I'd say so, Fabio. I wish he was more like you."

Chapter Nineteen

AT EIGHT-THIRTY THAT EVENING, MICHAEL and Fabio were cruising on Fabio's motorcycle down a narrow, tree-lined street as the sun made its final dash behind the distant hills.

"So where are we going?" said Michael.

Fabio leaned over on his bike and said, "I am taking you to a very quiet place that is classy and elegant. I think it is just the place you are needing."

Michael grinned and said, "Fabio, I thought pizza was it for tonight. Is this another part of the date?"

"You see?" said Fabio. "Life is not all bad, Michele. You still have your sense of humor."

The dark-eyed Italian led Michael to a brownstone in the middle of the street and tugged on the door's handle. Ushering Michael in, he quickly headed to the bar and said, "This is Cassiopeia. I think you will like it. There aren't too many people here. This bar is for grown-ups." He patted Michael on the back.

Cassiopeia's bartender, a tall, slender man of about thirty with a crew cut, stood facing his customers. His back was against a mirror with a shelf containing assorted spirits. He had one foot propped up on a case of wine. The bar was a sleek line of mahogany with a brass rail and foot rest. The mirror behind him was framed with terracotta tile that ran up to the ceiling. Various images of the recognizable, W-shaped constellation beamed down on the patrons who were bathed in the bar's subtle lighting. Michael instantly drew comfort from the warmth of the colors. The rich burgundies, deep oranges, and lusty ambers that slowly swirled around and around.

Fabio waved to the bartender as he and Michael passed, and the tall man nodded, wiping the inside of a tumbler. "Come, Michele, this way," said Fabio, leading him around a small, tight maze of shiny chrome and mirrored glass tables until they arrived at one in the corner.

A twenty-something waiter approached. He was tall, toned, and tanned, and his collar-length, jet black hair was streaked back with olive oil. He heard the men speaking in English and said, "What can I bring you?"

"Nothing yet," said Fabio. "We are waiting for friends."

Michael watched as the serious waiter nodded. He couldn't help notice the man's incredible good looks. And his clothes were far too neat for a waiter's, he thought. When the attractive-looking man turned and walked away, Michael glanced around the room and noticed the other waiters were all similar—dressed to a T and all very handsome. They were also all male. There were no female waitresses. And also the customers were male as well. He glanced at Fabio and said, "Fabio, this *is* another part of the date. And you brought me to a gay bar. I should have known, from the hair." He flipped the ends of Fabio's wavy locks.

Fabio shook his head and lifted his hair from his shoulders. "I knew you were jealous of my hair." He glanced around the bar. "But this is not the gay bar. It is simply classy. Do not worry, it is still early. The *signorine*, they will be here soon. You will see."

Michael shrugged and said, "Fabio, do you think one of the *signorine* that will come here tonight could be the one?"

"The one what?" He scanned the room.

"You know, the one for you, Miss Right," said Michael. "The one you'll spend your life with. Do you believe in that sort of thing?"

"*Absolutamente.* There is nothing more important in the life than *amore*, Michele. You know that."

He sighed. "Yeah, I know. But I don't just mean love. I mean the kind of love that consumes you. The kind that makes you burn with passion for her twenty-four hours a day, every day. The kind that makes you want her, and only her." He couldn't get the image of Camille out of his head. "Do you think that one will come tonight? And you will run away with her and spend your whole life with her?"

"I do believe in that kind of love, Michele," said Fabio. "And I am not sure if she will be here tonight, but someday." He formed his lips into a smirk and nodded. "Someday she will come. I am sure of it. I have always been imagining it. It will be somewhere we do not expect. We will meet under the stars," he gazed up at the painted ceiling and made a child-like smile, "on the beach. I have always loved the beach."

"Fabio, I had no idea you were such a romantic," said Michael. "Are you sure you're not trying to seduce me?"

And no sooner than Michael had said it, did the first wave of elegant ladies sweep in. Fabio nudged Michael with an elbow and wiggled his eyebrows. Seven elegant ladies walked by. And all were true ladies, dolled up in fancy, expensive evening gowns with lace and sequins. They wore sparkly purses and high heels showing off sexy ankles. One of the seven wore a wrap and Michael's eyes immediately flew to her, thinking about how elegant she must be to don the silk in that heat. The ladies sat at two tables pushed together by the waiters, and Fabio eyed the girl with the wrap. "That might be her," he said, winking. She was medium height, slender, with warm brown hair neatly tucked with a rhinestone butterfly hair clip on one side close to her head. Fabio clutched at his breast, making eye contact even before the girls had time to settle into their seats. Miss Silk Wrap smiled over at the men, and to Michael's surprise, she stood up and walked over to their table. Fabio drank her in and she said, "Do you have a cigarette?"

Fabio patted his chest and sighed a breath of relief when he felt the pack of cigarettes in his inside jacket pocket. He pulled it out, dug inside the pack, and pulled one of the last two cigarettes out. The young lady loosely twisted her wrap around one arm, reached for the cigarette and held it out between two slender fingers. Fabio dove into his pockets now for his lighter, but couldn't find it. He asked Michael, who reached into a pocket for his old lighter. When Michael remembered he had tossed the lighter aside in the cave, he shrugged at Fabio, but Fabio had located a box of matches in one of his pockets. Fabio struck the match and held it up to the cigarette's tip. The girl pulled her hand up to her lips and softly sucked until the tip went red. "I am Fabio," he said, his eyebrows riding up and down.

"Grazie," said the girl, releasing a small puff of white smoke towards his mouth. She offered him a hand. "Fabio. I like. *Molto* sexy," she said.

Fabio took the girl's hand in his, and her dancing, dark eyes drew him nearer and nearer. Just then, a party of four walked into the bar and headed to their table. A tall, brown-haired young man waved and then called to Fabio. "Ah, there are my friends," said Fabio, now waving back. He kissed Miss Silk Wrap's hand and said, "*Mi dispiace, signorina*. But my friends," indicating the small party with a nod. The girl twisted and spotted three beautiful, young girls following the tall man. She stroked Fabio's cheek, wiggled her fingers to wave goodbye, and made her way back to the table with the other six goddesses.

"Isn't that them?" said Michael, gesturing over to the seven pretty ladies. "I thought those were the ones."

Fabio chuckled as he shook his head, placed a hand on Michael's forearm and said, "Michele, seven is too many. Even for Fabio."

Michael now spotted Fabio's friend who waved. Trailing the tall gentleman, the three ravishing beauties slid into view as they made their way over to the table. Fabio greeted the four newcomers and began introductions. Gennaro was a pleasant and positive man who worked as a hotel concierge in Rome, but at a different hotel than where Fabio worked. Gina, his girlfriend, also worked there.

"Michele, I want you to meet Chiara," he said. "She is my girlfriend." A perfume girl at Coin department store, Chiara had been Fabio's girlfriend for only a month, sharing the title with two other young pretties in that same month. Fabio kissed both of her cheeks and then wrapped an arm around her neck and tiny shoulder. Though she wore extremely high heels, the top of her head barely reached Fabio's collar bone.

Michael extended a hand to the young woman, but Fabio corrected him. "Michele, I told you before, we do not shake hands in *Italia*, especially with *le ragazze, eh?*"

So Michael hesitantly spread his arms out and tiny Chiara filled them. They kissed each other on both cheeks.

Then Fabio gestured to the final member of the party, a young woman of medium height with raven hair. He looked at Michael, smiled and raised his eyebrows. "And Michele,

Chiara has brought her friend along," he said. "Now it is all even, three boys and three girls, yes? Her name is Fiorella." Fabio peered at Michael, to make sure he would not mess up the greeting again.

Michael took hold of the girl and gave her the customary kiss on each cheek. As they parted, he took in her beauty, buxom and curvaceous, and her figure-hugging, short, black dress and black high heels. Her very full, ruby lips screamed sensuality.

As they took their seats, Fabio leaned in close to Michael and said, "I told you, Michele, it is classy here. And not the gay bar." He then called for the chic waiter to bring a bottle of prosecco.

"Right," said Michael, and turned back to the young woman next to him. Long, straight, flaxen hair played off the shiny black dress, and white pearls were strung around her smooth neck. Her tiny nose and inviting, grey-green eyes made his loins ache. She was absolutely stunning, and he thought that any red-blooded American guy would have died for this chance with her. The young lady turned to him and, resting her elbow on the glass table, and bent her hand backwards. She spread apart two of her fingers, curled the others into her palm and said, "You do have a cigarette, yes?"

Michael hissed at Fabio "Pssst, Fabio, cigarette," he said, with one beckoning hand.

Fabio pulled the pack from his pocket again and tossed it across the table. Michael handed the pack's last cigarette to the girl. Fabio tossed him the box of matches. He ran his thumb along the striker and Fiorella puffed on the cigarette's filter. "Grazie," she said, with pouty lips, like a baby sucking. "You speak *Italiano*, no?"

"*Un po'*."

"You *do* know *amore*, yes?" She grinned and blew a tiny puff of white smoke into his face.

"Oh, yes, I know *amore*," he said.

The waiter arrived with the prosecco and six champagne flutes, popped the cork and poured. Fabio toasted to everyone's health, and the bubbly liquid went down quickly. As the waiter ambled by again, Gennaro ordered a round of Campari and sodas for the table. After more toasting, the two Italian men downed their cocktails, with Michael watching and following next. A second round of cocktails arrived with a couple of platters of appetizers, one of meats and cheeses and fish, and the other with roasted vegetables. The second crisp, bitter drink went down more slowly now as everyone picked at the hors d'oeuvres.

Fabio waved a hand across the table and said, "Michele, tell my friends about your *famiglia*."

Michael turned to him and spoke as if the others were not at the table. "But I can't explain all that in Italian. It's too much," he said.

"Don't worry," he said. "All my friends, they are speaking the English, too." Fabio tapped him on the cheek.

Gennaro smiled across the table and said, "Yes, don't worry, my *americano* friend."

Michael shrugged, and told them about how his father had been stationed in Italy during the war, how he had met Caterina and they had fallen in love. He explained how this story all led to Michael's quest to find his half-brother. The party remained quiet all through the telling. Fabio nodded his head knowingly and confidently, like he had no doubt that they would soon find the lost relative.

Gennaro was not so sure. "But Michele," he said, "how do you find him, with no more leads, eh?"

"I don't know," said Michael. "It seems to get harder than easier." He sighed.

Fabio slapped Michael on the back. "Hey, come on, Michele. Do not give up, ah? I promise you, we will find him."

"Yes, you did, Fabio," said Michael, now only half believing it himself.

After a first round of a rich and full-bodied red wine from a vineyard in Tuscany, the conversation turned. Wishing to think about his dilemma no longer, Michael asked about their interests and the members of the party took turns relaying the information. Gennaro liked to travel with Gina, and talked about a recent trip to Paris. *Paris*, thought Michael, with a shudder, *how strange and coincidental*. Then Gennaro also told him about the one time he had gone to New York. Fabio spoke about how he and Gennaro often went skiing in the Italian Alps. And the girls spoke briefly about food and fashion in Italy.

Fabio landed a kiss on Chiara's upper arm and looked up at Michael. "Do not be shy, Michele," he said, hinting over at Fiorella with a nod. "*Italia*, she is a country of lovers. And you are *Italiano*. It is in your blood." The swarthy Fabio continued smooching up his girl's arm adding romantic whisperings in her ear, until he realized it was making Michael uncomfortable.

He pulled away from Chiara, gestured over to Fiorella, and said to Michael, "You do not like her?"

"Oh, no, she's beautiful," said Michael. "She's very sweet and very sexy. She's just not —"

"Not what?" said Fabio.

"She's just not."

"Oh, I see," said Fabio, "she's not the girl from your room."

He squinted hard at Fabio "What are you talking about?" Then Michael turned to Fiorella and, indicating Fabio, said, "He's drunk. He doesn't know what he's talking about. There's no girl in my room."

Fiorella inched away from Michael and said, "If you are Italian like Fabio, then yes, there *is* a girl in your room."

"Never mind what he says," said Michael.

Just then Cecilia and Camille walked in and the bartender directed them over to Fabio's table.

Fabio stood and raised his arm. "Ah, look who it is," he said. "Cecilia and Camilla. Come, come." He waved them closer. "Gennaro, pull up some chairs for them."

"We did not expect you," said Fabio. "But how nice you are now here. It was a complete surprise."

"Right. Complete surprise," said Michael.

Fabio's Italian friends all knew Cecilia from the hotel. They greeted each other as Italians did, and then Cecilia and Camille joined everyone at the table. Cecilia sat next to Fabio and Camille sat next to Cecilia, across from Michael and Fiorella.

Camille stared across the table at Michael. "You missed an excellent bucatini amatriciana, my darling," she said. "Too bad."

"Rub it in, why don't you?" said Michael.

Fabio blocked one side of his mouth with his hand and, indicating Camille, whispered to Fiorella, "The girl from his room."

"Ah," said Fiorella as she nodded. She looked at Camille. "There is *always* a girl in the room. Michele is *Italiano* like Fabio."

Camille sized up Fiorella. She immediately knew what Fiorella was. Or what she imagined her to be. A man-stealing hussy. *But Michael is not my man to steal,* she thought. Still, it irked her. Camille wanted to want him. She wanted Michael to be her man. But Claude was always there, in the back of her mind. And so was their impending wedding. She also wanted to hate Fiorella.

"I don't think Michael is anything like Fabio," said Camille.

"Camille, you need a drink," said Cecilia. She called for the waiter.

He approached the table already carrying another bottle of the red wine from Tuscany and two more glasses. He poured for Camille and Cecilia.

Chiara had a sip of her wine. "I do," she said.

Fabio twisted at the shoulders and looked at her. "You do what?" he asked.

"I think you and Michele are the same," said Chiara. She glanced from Fabio to Michael. "You are even the same size."

"We are not," said Fabio. He added a dismissing wave of his hand to his protesting tone.

"Are you sure?" asked Chiara.

Avoiding the subject, Fabio winked at Michael and said, "Michele, you have not touched your wine."

"That's not true. Look," said Michael, lifting the glass from the table. It was half-filled.

Gennaro glared at him and said, "That is not drinking. You have to learn, my *americano* friend."

"What is there to learn? It's a glass of wine. And I am drinking it."

With a smile up one side of his face and a shake of his head, Fabio said, "Michele, your face, it tells the story. It is a sad story. And life should not be sad. You must learn *il dolce far niente*. You must learn to live *Italiano*, like we live."

His reply was a deep sigh.

Gennaro lifted his wine glass. "To live *Italiano* means to enjoy life," he said. Gina raised her glass and gazed over at Michael, sending a pleasant smile to him while taking a small sip of wine.

Michael lifted his glass and swirled the wine for all at the table to see. "Like this?" he asked. Then he drank.

"Yes, but you must learn more from your friend Fabio," said Gennaro. Then a thought popped into his mind. "Hey, I know what would be fun," he said.

"Ooh. A game?" asked Cecilia.

"*Si*. A game," said Gennaro. "Let's play a game."

"I love games," said Gina. "I want to play."

"Yes, we will all play," said Gennaro.

"All right, what's the game?" asked Camille.

Gennaro smirked. "Our new *americano* friend Michele has told us his sad story of his father and his father's first love Caterina. And when his father left *Italia*, he left Caterina with a big belly. The baby was a boy, and he never knew his father. Now, we will play the game what if our *Italiano* friend Fabio is Caterina's son?"

"What?!" said Fabio. "Gennaro, it is not possible. And this does not sound like a fun game."

"I think it is fun," said Gina.

"Me too," said Fiorella. "I would love if Michele and Fabio were brothers." She squeezed closer to Michael and snuggled under his arm. "We could do many things together." Then she glared across the table at Camille.

"I can't imagine what 'things' you would do," said Camille. She glared back at Fiorella. "Michael is not the kind of man you think he is."

"Do *you* know what kind of man he is, Camilla?" asked Cecilia.

Camille didn't reply. She watched Fiorella nuzzle against Michael's chest. Then she turned her face away from them.

And Cecilia said, "I think you know."

"It is a big possibility," said Gennaro. "Fabio, you are the right age. You have no other brother or sister. You have black hair and Michele has black hair. You have the same dark eyes. And even the nose is the same."

"*Si*," said Cecilia. "I can see a resemblance."

"No, no!" said Fabio. "There is no resemblance. My hair is long. Michele's hair is so short."

"You are funny, Fabio," said Gina.

"*Si*, very funny," said Gennaro. He stared into Fabio's eyes and turned his head slightly to the side. "And Fabio, you have never told us about your father."

"What is there to tell?" said Fabio. "A father is a father." His cheeks flushed.

"Fabio, you *are* funny," said Gennaro. "It was only a game. Do not worry. We know you are not Michele's brother." He waved his hands over the table. "We all have brothers. How would you feel if you had one?"

"I don't know," said Fabio. "But I am glad everyone knows Michele is not mine. Because I do not want to disappoint him anymore."

Michael chuckled. "Don't worry, Fabio. We're friends. And you can't disappoint me."

"*Bene*," said Fabio. Because I have much more to teach you, as a friend."

Michael nodded.

During a brief silent moment, the oil-slicked waiter returned with more food. White plates contained steaming dishes of eggplant parmigiano, spaghetti alla carbonara, bucatini and sardines, seared lamb, steamed artichokes, fried calamari, sea urchins, and anchovies drenched in olive oil. He set them down with hunks of fresh rustic bread and savory cheese. Every inch of the glass table was covered. Michael and Camille looked on, stunned at the enormous amount of food.

Fabio reached for a slab of pecorino cheese and a plump artichoke. "You see, Michele," he said, pointing to the many dishes, "this is *il dolce far niente*. She is *molto bella*."

Chiara smiled over to Michael and with a raised glass said, "*Il dolce far niente*."

Gennaro and Gina followed in the same manner.

Michael, testing out the bucatini and sardines, said, "But what does it mean?"

Fabio grinned and said, "She means we eat, we drink, we laugh, we love. She means to be *Italiano*."

Nodding along with Fabio's still perplexing explanation, Michael said, "I think I understand." He thrust forward his glass, raising it to the others, and downed the deep, red liquid. He laughed along with the group. It was happening slowly, but they were witnessing the Italian seed in him beginning to germinate.

As the group shared more of the Italian way of life with their new friends, the three young girls asked about American life, American movies and television, and Hollywood stars.

What was it like to live with the world's most famous actors and beautiful models? What were American girls like? And American men? One after another, Michael and Camille batted the questions like badminton birdies, finally getting their point across that it was much harder to meet a famous person than they had thought.

As the plates continued to pile up and the wine continued to flow, the giddy party shared stories, hugs, and lots of laughter. Michael shared personal feelings with these newfound friends—passions, longings, even regrets. He found himself—whether it was from the wine or not he could not tell—opening up to them, and was able to say things to these Italians that he had had trouble saying to anyone back home in New York. Like a bear emerging from his months of hibernation, Michael felt good about waking to a new life. Among these people, he felt good to be alive.

As for Camille, she also felt good to be alive. Like Michael, she felt good to drink in the enticing aromas of the Italian dishes and the hearty sweetness of the wine like it was the very first time. She enjoyed hearing the genuine laughter and cheerful conversation of the other patrons, and to see the sparkle in their honest eyes. She somehow knew that it was something more than just Italian wine that flowed through the veins of these straightforward, warm Italians. It was their Italian spirit that shone through them and their lust for life that emanated from within. The only thing Camille didn't feel good about was the way Fiorella threw herself at Michael.

And like Camille, Michael also lapped up the Italian spirit, and his sorrows all vanished, replaced with this inexorable, exuberant feeling that was washing over him like tiny ripples in a steaming hot tub. He wanted to soak his aching bones and muscles in the sweet warm waters of "doing nothing". And thanks to these wildly free and life-loving Italians, now he knew how.

Michael shifted away from Fiorella. He looked at the others. "You have all taught me a great deal tonight," he said. "I feel like I was with good friends that I've known for a very long time. *Grazie.*"

"I know what you are saying," said Fabio.

"And now it's time to go," said Michael. He stood and reached over the table for Camille's hand. He looked at Fabio and said, "Thank you for tonight, Fabio."

Fabio smiled and said, "*Prego.* What are friends for?"

Michael tapped Fabio on the shoulder. He squeezed Camille's hand and they left.

Fiorella rounded the table and squeezed up against Fabio. She looked at him and asked, "I did good? Was I convincing?"

Fabio pulled her under his arm, smiled and said, "You did great." He kissed her on her forehead.

"Yes, you were great, Fiorella," said Cecilia. "But we still have more to do if they are going to fall in love for true."

Chapter Twenty

MICHAEL WALKED OUT OF THE BATHROOM with a white towel wrapped around his waist. His hair was wet and wavy. He made his way to the closet. Camille was sitting at a small table looking into a hand-held mirror. She wore a white dress with a pastel flower print that reached mid-thigh. She adjusted her makeup and spotted him passing behind her in the mirror.

"Last night was fun," said Michael.

Camille turned and eyed his physique with curiosity. His back muscles swelled as he reached into the closet. "Yes, it was," she said.

Michael turned holding a pair of grey trousers and a blue shirt. He looked at Camille. "What'd you think of Fabio's friends?" he asked. "Nice, right?"

"More than nice," said Camille. She picked up a brush from the table and slowly brushed her long hair. "They were all so warm and accepting and full of life."

"I thought so too," said Michael. "I've never met people like that. They take you in to their circle without batting an eye."

"I know," said Camille. "They were all so very welcoming and warm. Except for that Fiorella."

"What was wrong with Fiorella?" asked Michael. "I thought she was very nice." He walked into the bathroom, dropped the towel and pulled on his trousers. Then he slipped on his blue shirt.

"Yeah, a little *too* nice," said Camille.

Michael combed his hair and came out of the bathroom again. "What?"

"I said she was a little too nice. That Fiorella," said Camille. "She was a little too Italian."

"What does that mean?" asked Michael. He tucked his shirt into his trousers.

"It means, my pet, that she was a little too close for comfort," said Camille.

"Oh, that," said Michael. He chuckled. "Yes, well, I think that may have been Fabio's doing."

"Fabio?" said Camille.

"Right," said Michael. "You know Fabio. He was just playing a little game."

"There were a lot of games going on last night, my darling," said Camille.

"Yes, well, I wouldn't make anything of it," said Michael. "Fiorella was beautiful and sexy. But she wasn't for me."

"Oh?" said Camille. She felt a wave of relief pass through her. She looked at Michael. "That's good."

Michael's eyes went wide. But before he could reply, Camille said, "I mean, it's good that you're not one of those men who focus on beauty on the outside."

"No, I'm not," he said.

"Yes. Well, I knew you weren't," said Camille.

"Don't worry," said Michael. "They were just games."

"Right. Just games," said Camille. "I must confess. I'm a little glad the games ended."

"Me too," he said. Michael inched closer to her and grabbed her by the elbows. "And today, it's just going to be you and me. We're going to see the sights that made Rome great."

"Really? Just you and me?" asked Camille. "What about Fabio?"

"I certainly couldn't say no to Fabio," said Michael. "After all, he's done so much for me. For us."

"Of course."

"And it was his idea," said Michael. "How he scolded me when I told him I hadn't seen anything in Rome except cafés and bars. It's disgraceful. I admit it." Michael walked over to the night stand. He reached for his watch and his wallet.

"I'll go along with you there," said Camille. "I'm not used to not seeing the main attractions. It's a good thing we are going. I can bring my camera and finally get some decent shots of Rome."

"A grand idea," said Michael. He watched her as she wiggled in the small chair. "Hey, you ought to get ready, my sweet."

"I *am* ready," said Camille. She turned back to the mirror and looked at her face. Then she looked at him. "You can be very rude sometimes. You know that, my pet?"

Michael knew she didn't mean it. She had said, "my pet," and whenever that happened, it was all just another game. Although, he worried if Camille had half-meant it and that maybe she was only trying to put him in his place. To remind him that, although she was changing and becoming more accepting of other ways at looking at life, she was still a proud and confident woman who could stand on her own two feet.

And Michael knew he had to change too. He was now happier than he had been in a great long while, but very glad that Camille was around to make sure he would stay that way.

"I'm sorry, my sweet," he said. "Let's get out of here. What do you say?"

Camille stood and reached for her purse that was on the bed. She slipped by him and waltzed toward the door. "Way ahead of you, my pet," she said.

Chapter Twenty-One

EVEN THOUGH MICHAEL HAD NEVER HAD any intention of going to Italy before finding out he had a half-brother, he had long wondered what the Coliseum would really be like. Television pictures could show what it looked like, but wasn't there much more to it than that? With Camille and Fabio, he now stood tall on a thick marble floor that circled away on both sides. All three gazed in many directions to take in the enormous structure.

"I am so happy you chose the *Colosseo*, Michele," said Fabio. "Many, many people come to see it every day. But it is still a favorite place of mine. There is no other place in *Italia* with this kind of power."

"Power's a good word for it, Fabio," said Michael. "I can almost sense a fight coming on."

"Oh, you are such a big joker, Michele," said Fabio. He slapped Michael on the shoulder.

Fabio lifted his head. "Let's go up higher," he said.

"All right," said Michael.

The two men and Camille climbed up one level and stood against a metal guard rail. They peered down to what once was the stage. Where all the bloody battles had taken place in Rome's heyday. It now contained wooden slats that provided a visual portrayal of what the arena would have looked like in Rome's ancient time. Camille arched her neck and let out a squeal, her emotions running away with her.

"What was that for?" asked Michael. But he really thought, *Oh, how I have missed her laugh. Did I really used to think it was annoying?*

"Just excited, that's all," she said.

"You are funny, Camilla," said Fabio.

Michael chuckled. "I thought maybe you wanted to see if those people on the other side could hear you," he said.

"That would be fun," said Camille.

"You want to shriek again?" asked Michael. "Come on. A really big shout. Give it your best shot."

"No," said Camille. "I want to run around to the other side and laugh really loud. And then you see if you can hear me from all the way over there. Like a game."

"I thought you had enough of games," said Michael.

Camille smiled sinfully. "I changed my mind."

"All right," said Michael.

"You *are* funny, Camilla," said Fabio.

Michael pressed his hand to Camille's shoulder. "You go around to the other side and we'll listen for your cackle," he said.

Michael looked at Fabio. "All right, Fabio?"

Fabio nodded. "I can listen," he said.

"I don't cackle," said Camille. "I laugh."

"All right, we'll listen for your laugh," said Michael. "Just hurry up and go."

"All right," said Camille. "And I'll snap a picture of you two from the other side. It'll be fun."

Michael looked at his wristwatch. "I'll time you," he said. "Ready. Set. Go!"

Camille darted away to the right. In about three minutes, she was on the far side of the arena, exactly opposite Michael and Fabio.

"How long did she take?" asked Fabio.

Michael looked up from his watch. "I don't know. I wasn't really timing her," he said. "And I lost her. Do you see her?"

"No, I do not see her either," said Fabio. "Do you think she fell down to the arena and a big lion ate her?"

"That's not funny, Fabio," said Michael.

"Michele?" said Fabio.

"Ok. It's a little funny," said Michael. "But I still don't see her."

They continued to gaze across the wide expanse, but could not spot her. Camille had slipped between two groups of tourists. It was a tight squeeze. But she jumped up and down with her hands in the air. And they still could not see her.

Camille stopped jumping. She leaned forward and positioned her camera on a metal rail. She peered across the arena and she too could not spot Michael or Fabio. Then she looked into her viewfinder. She searched for them while adjusting her zoom lens. And just when she thought she had spotted Michael, a couple of tourists passed in front of him, blocking Michael from Camille's view. The man was elderly. He accidently bumped into Michael and dropped his camera. Michael bent down to retrieve it for the older man just as Camille looked into her viewfinder a second time. She now saw no one. So she moved her camera and this time thought she spotted Fabio. Just then, the other tourist, the older woman stood in front of Fabio. And again, Camille's view was blocked. She moved her camera around and still couldn't find Michael or Fabio.

Just then, Michael called to her across the arena. "My darling!" he bellowed. "I'm here!" He waved his hands in the air. And then she knew.

Camille pointed her camera at the shouting man. She confirmed it was Michael jumping up and down. So she did the same. She jumped and waved her arms wildly. He finally spotted her. "Over there," he said to Fabio. He pointed straight across the arena. "She's over there."

Fabio pointed his eyes at the spot. "I see her!" he said. "I see our Camilla!" And then he jumped and waved his hands high in the air.

Camille held her camera high for them to see and then brought it to one eye. She focused the lens and then zoomed their figures closer. In her excitement, her finger slipped on the lens and the image of Michael's face came very large into her view. He looked like a dreamer. A confident man very hopeful about the future. A trustworthy man who wanted more out of life than he had. He looked like a man in love. Camille didn't know how she knew all this from a single quick peek at him. She just knew that she knew. Camille reduced the zoom and caught both Michael and Fabio in the lens now. She quickly snapped a picture and then drew the camera away from her eye. She stepped back and steadied herself against a huge marble stump. *But just who is he in love with?* she wondered. Overwhelmed with the image of Michael's expression, Camille forgot to laugh.

The Pantheon was minutes from the Colosseum. The walk was leisurely. It was too hot to move any faster. Michael suggested they stop for a coffee or gelato before going any further. But Fabio shot that idea down. He insisted that they go to a very famous café near the Pantheon. "The café with the best espresso in *Roma*," were his words.

"Do they have anything cold?" asked Camille.

"*Si. Certo,*" said Fabio. "*Granita.* Iced espresso. You will love, Camilla."

"Great."

"But after. First we go to the Pantheon," said Fabio. "There you will see something you will never see any place else."

"All right," said Camille. "Count me in."

They turned onto a narrow street. Crowds of people were squeezed everywhere trying to make their way in both directions. The street was lined on both sides with cafés, restaurants and souvenir shops, but especially with churches.

"I have never seen so many churches on one block," said Camille. "And in places you'd never expect. Squeezed between houses and shops. Every few buildings. Who would put a church there, it makes you wonder."

"*Si,*" said Fabio.

"Why so many, Fabio?" she asked.

Fabio shrugged. "This is *Roma,*" he said. "She has many churches because we are so close to God."

"All right. I'll accept that," said Camille.

They plodded along the narrow street with its congested buildings until it finally opened up into a bustling space. It was like the three of them were water squeezing through the neck of a very full bottle. Then the Pantheon burst into view. All of a sudden, they were standing in a square large enough to hold a thousand Romans. And staring up at the old structure. It was a very large and very round building with rows of marble columns on the portico holding up a triangle of marble near the entrance. And it was obvious that everything around it had come much later.

Michael knocked his elbow into Camille's. "Hey, I couldn't hear your laugh," he said. "You know, your laugh."

"I didn't laugh," said Camille. "Who would laugh at this?" She pointed at the round building.

"I don't mean now," he said. "At the Colosseum. When you were on the other side."

"Yes, well. I guess I forgot," said Camille.

"Doesn't sound like you," he said. "I didn't think you forgot anything, my pet."

"I do," said Camille. "But only sometimes, my darling. When I must."

"All right," said Michael. "And I'll accept that."

He faced Fabio. "Do we go right in?" he asked.

"*Si*, Michele," said Fabio. "There is no mass now. So we go right in. *Andiamo*." He waved his hand.

There were only a handful of people inside. It was strange to see it. Outside tourists crowded the streets and the massive square. Inside was a calm haven for worshippers of all beliefs. And for non-worshippers too. It didn't matter what you believed. The Pantheon let you believe in it.

Fabio quickly pointed out the oculus in the center of the rotunda's coffered concrete dome. Bright sunlight streaked through the large opening forming a fanning beam that flooded white light onto the geometric shapes of the marble floor. Camille and Michael stood awestruck for a moment.

"But look," said Fabio. "There." He tugged on Michael's arm.

Michael and Camille followed him to one stretch of the rotunda's perimeter. Catholic statues and paintings and busts, later additions to the once Roman temple, were scattered about. Fabio directed them to the third niche and pointed out a sarcophagus behind glass. "Do you know who is there?" he asked.

Michael and Camille both shrugged.

"Raffaello," said Fabio.

"Raffaello?" asked Michael.

"The artist," said Fabio.

"Oh, wow. Raphael," said Camille. "I can't believe it. He's so great."

"Yes, he is right there," said Fabio. "What is left of him. His bones and ashes."

"That's something," said Michael.

Fabio pointed to a memorial plaque on the sarcophagus. "Can you read it, Michele?"

Michael scoffed. "Of course not."

"I am a poor teacher," said Fabio. "You do not learn fast enough, Michele."

"Yes, well," said Michael. "What does it say?"

Fabio scanned the Italian words. He said, "Raffaello is lying here. Bones and ashes. While he was alive, he tried to overcome Mother Nature. When he died, Nature died too. Something like that."

"Whoa." Michael stroked his chin slowly.

"His lady is here too," said Fabio.

"His lady?" asked Camille.

"Fiancée," said Fabio. "She is named Maria. She died before they could marry."

"Oh, no," said Camille. She reached her hand up to her chest and twisted her white dress near her heart. "That's so sad."

"*Si,*" said Fabio. "It is very sad when two people in love cannot be together. But at least they can be together now."

"I guess it teaches us an important lesson," said Michael.

"What is that, Michele?" asked Fabio.

Michael looked at Camille. "That we shouldn't wait. We should tell the people we love that we love them. Every day. And we should not waste even one day being apart from them. Life is too precious. And love is too important."

Fabio put his hand on Michael's shoulder. "You are learning, Michele," he said. "You are becoming *Italiano*. Maybe you are almost there."

Michael chuckled. "Yeah. Maybe," he said.

Just then, the white light from the oculus that had been shining so brightly on the geometric floor began to fade. It turned a dark grey and then it vanished. And just as quickly, a strong rain began to fall through the oculus. Hard droplets pinged on the marble floor.

"I have never seen this before," said Fabio.

"Never?" asked Michael.

"Never," said Fabio. "But do not worry. All the rain, she will stay in the center."

"What do you mean?" asked Michael.

"This building was made in ancient times," said Fabio. "People were smart then. They made this place smart. When it rains, the rain falls to the floor in the center. But it stays there. It does not spread out to the ends. The floor goes down in the center, so if we stay on the end, we will not get wet."

"Is that true?" asked Camille. "Or is that you just being funny, Fabio?"

"No, no. It is true, Camilla," said Fabio.

As they looked on, the rain continued to fall through the large opening in the dome, but it collected in the center of the rotunda. The water poured down. But it did not spread beyond a few feet from the center of the floor.

"That's good enough for me," said Camille. She slipped her shoulder out from under her camera strap. Then she handed the camera to Michael. "Here. Take my picture," she said.

"What? I don't know how to use this thing," he said.

"Just point it at me and press this button," she said. She pointed to the shutter.

"Now?" he asked.

"No. Wait," said Camille. "Let me get into position." Then she removed her high heels, left them at Michael's feet and ran to the center of the rotunda. Water streamed down upon Camille. She lifted her head and stroked her arms and body as if she was lapping up the refreshing wetness of a tropical waterfall.

"Now!" she called over to Michael.

Camille posed with her limbs stretched out and fingers and toes curled like a muse waiting for her favorite artist to paint her. Michael looked into the viewfinder and snapped a few pictures. Then, with her face to the sky, Camille brushed back her dark hair with long strokes of her hands. She let her hands fall to her sides and let the rain soak through her white dress. She waited for Michael to snap another picture. Then she composed herself and joined Michael and Fabio.

"That was…something," said Michael.

"*Si. Molto bene*," said Fabio. "Very good, Camilla. *Brava*! You are like a beautiful movie star.'"

Moments later, they gazed up at the oculus in the dome. The rain had stopped and the sun had returned to the sky. And the bright white beam streamed through the opening once again.

Fabio shook his head. "I have never seen it before," he said. "It must have been some sort of miracle."

"Some sort," said Camille. She laughed. But quietly this time. "Now, Fabio, I recall you owe me an iced espresso," she said. She wrapped her arm around his shoulder and they walked toward the exit with Michael silently following.

Again the sun was bearing down on Rome. And it didn't take long for Camille, or Fabio's left shoulder, to dry off. A two-minute walk around the western end of the Pantheon led them to the Sant' Eustachio Il Caffé. It was geographically hidden within a tiny street in a constantly crowded part of Rome. But every Roman knew how to find it. They knew the one thing about the café that drew so many customers: their espresso, heralded as the best in all of Rome. Just as Fabio had said. He beamed a wide smile when the colorful sign came into view.

"There it is, Camilla," said Fabio. "We can know enjoy the best coffee in *Roma*."

"Coffee? I thought you said espresso ice," said Camille.

"What do you think makes the espresso ice?" asked Fabio.

Camille jerked her elbow at Michael. "Fabio, you've been hanging around with this one too long," she said.

"I am sorry, Camilla," said Fabio. "I was only joking."

"I know. It's ok."

"The truth is that we *Italiano* call espresso *caffe*."

"That could be confusing," said Camille.

"Not for us," said Fabio.

"So when do we get to taste this, what did you call it?" asked Michael.

"*Granita*," said Fabio. "And we taste it right away. I go and order them now."

But there was a line of customers and they had to wait outside. There wasn't much break from the scorching sun. It beat down on them hard. They tried to huddle under the café's one awning. Two other customers squeezed next to Michael, pushing him into Camille, who pushed into Fabio. The customers laughed with embarrassment and apologized.

Michael brushed it off and smiled at them. Camille cackled. Then Michael turned his face toward Camille. Her face was already very close to his, and Michael accidentally brushed his nose against Camille's. They smelled each other. Then their eyes met. Michael wanted to kiss her. He could think of only that. But Camille giggled a nervous laugh. Michael breathed it in. "This is so silly," he said.

"What is, my darling?" asked Camille. She looked deep into his eyes.

Fabio was squished up against Camille. He stretched his head over Camille's shoulder. "Are you all right, Camilla?" he asked.

"Oh, yes," she said. "I'm fine. Never better."

"Just be careful about Michele," said Fabio. "He is almost being whole *Italiano*. That means a true lover."

Camille kept looking into Michael's eyes. But she spoke to Fabio. "I think I'll be all right. I'm a big girl."

I'll say, thought Michael.

About ten minutes later, the three of them were standing under the blazing sun and quickly crunching their way through their iced espressos.

"Fabio, it's really good," said Camille. She dabbed her finger at some coffee dripping down her chin.

Fabio nodded. "Good, yes?" he asked.

"The best in Rome?" asked Camille.

"The best," said Fabio. He licked his finger and used it to wipe the coffee from Camille's chin.

Then he looked past Camille at Michael. "Michele, what do you think?" he asked. "You like the *granita*?"

"Hmm? Oh, yeah," said Michael. "It's a nice day. A little hot though."

Fabio and Camille stared at Michael. "Are you ok, Michele?" asked Fabio.

But Michael didn't answer. His mind was still on Camille. And just how much of a big girl she was.

Chapter Twenty-Two

CAMILLE SQUEEZED BETWEEN MICHAEL and Fabio as they walked along the narrow street. There was an endless row of old homes, restaurants, cafés and shops. Camille linked one arm around Fabio's arm and the other around Michael's. And she wiggled her head so her hair would fall back and away from her face. A long strand dangled in front of her eye. She blew it up and away from her face. "What should we do next?" asked Camille.

"Whatever you wish," said Fabio.

"Yes," said Michael. "I recall someone here calling this week her week of freedom."

"Me!" cried Camille. "It was me."

"So, what's it going to be?" asked Michael. "Saint Peter's Church?"

Camille shook her head.

"The Mouth of Truth?" asked Michael.

"I'm pretty sure telling the truth should never be included in any week of freedom," said Camille. "Right, Fabio?"

"You are right, Camilla," said Fabio. "Oh, I know." Fabio snapped his fingers. "The Sistine Chapel. Everyone who comes to Rome must see the Sistine Chapel. Michelangelo was the best of all the great artists we have in *Italia*. And the ceiling of the Sistine Chapel proves it."

"No, no, no," said Camille. "I'd like to see something a little more, I don't know. I'm looking for a little fun. It's my week of freedom, remember?"

"The Spanish Steps," said Michael. "You could be just like Audrey Hepburn. We could have lunch there."

"Michele, we cannot eat at the Spanish Steps," said Fabio.

"Really?"

Fabio shook his head. "It is not allowed."

"But I thought—" said Michael.

"Michele, that was a movie," said Fabio. "Anything is possible in a movie. It is not real life. Real life is real life. Not a movie."

Camille turned to Fabio. "So you don't believe anything is possible in real life?"

"No, I did not say that," said Fabio. "Camilla, we cannot eat on the Spanish Steps if the *Roma polizia* says we cannot. That is real. But in real life, we can make the impossible possible. We can do things that movie people could never ever dream of doing."

"Like what?" asked Michael.

"Anything we want," said Fabio. "I will give you an example."

"Isn't that what I just asked for?" asked Michael.

"Oh, Michele, sometimes you are so serious," said Fabio.

"Get on with it already," said Michael. But Fabio didn't understand that statement. And so he didn't reply. "The example, Fabio."

"Ah, *si*," said Fabio. "We can make people do things they do not want to do. Things they do not *know* that they want to do."

"What?" asked Michael. "That doesn't make sense."

"Of course it does," said Fabio. "I will show you. I can make you eat gelato even if you do not have the idea of gelato in your silly head."

"Go on," said Michael. "Get out of here."

"I show you," said Fabio. "Did you think of eating gelato one minute ago?"

"No."

"But you do now," said Fabio. "Now you want to eat gelato."

Michael paused in thought, and then he realized that Fabio was right. All Fabio had done was say the word "gelato" and now Michael wanted to have some. "That's a nasty trick," said Michael.

"But it worked, yes, Michele?" asked Fabio.

"It worked."

"You did not even know you wanted gelato until I reminded you that you did," said Fabio.

"Like I said, a nasty trick," said Michael.

Then Camille asked, "Fabio, can you do that with other things?"

"*Si. Certo*," said Fabio. "I can do that magic trick with anything. In real life, I can make anything possible. Even falling in love when you did not know you wanted to fall in love."

"That's a little dangerous, Fabio, don't you think?" asked Camille.

"*Si,*" said Fabio. "But what is real life without a little danger?" He smirked.

"I've got it!" cried Camille.

"You want me I make you fall in love?" asked Fabio.

"Cut that out," she said. "I know where we should go next."

"Where?" asked Michael.

"The Trevi Fountain," said Camille. "I just have to go."

"Ok," said Michael. Then he asked, "But why do you want to go there?"

"To toss a coin in, my darling," she answered. "Why else?"

"Do you *have* any coins?" asked Michael. He knew she wouldn't have any. She was too much of a lady to carry coins.

"Of course not, my darling," said Camille. "I will toss *your* coins of course."

"Of course," he said.

"It is a great idea," said Fabio.

Michael asked Fabio, "You can get us there, Fabio. Can't you?"

"*Certo*," said Fabio. "We will see the Trevi Fountain in ten seconds. After this building."

He pointed to a small brown building on the corner and as soon as they walked past it, the Trevi Fountain came into view.

"There she is," said Fabio. He pointed at the fountain.

There was Neptune in all his glory, flanked by two hard-working Tritons and sheets of cascading water.

"How did you do that?" asked Camille.

"Just a little magic," said Fabio.

"I think you really *can* do magic, Fabio," said Camille.

"*Absolutamente*," said Fabio. "Can't you?"

Camille giggled and Michael perked up. "He's not magic," said Michael. "He's just very lucky."

"*Si,*" said Fabio. "Magic and luck too."

Camille smiled at Fabio. "And good looks too," she said. "It seems you have the whole package, Fabio." Then she looked at Michael and added, "I like that in a man."

Camille slipped her camera from her shoulder. "Stand over there," she said to the two men. Fabio and Michael moved to the spot. It was on the first level of steps in front of the rushing water. "Turn around."

"How's this?" Michael wrapped his arm around Fabio's shoulder.

"Great. Now stand still," said Camille.

Camille snapped two pictures of them in front of Neptune.

Then Michael nudged Fabio with his elbow. "Hey, Fabio, make a face like this," he said. Michael scrunched his face into a knot and stuck out his tongue.

"Ok, Michele," said Fabio. "I try." Fabio copied Michael's silly face and yelled to Camille, "You like this one?"

"Beautiful," she called back. "You never looked better." She snapped the picture and then cackled.

It warmed Michael's heart. He wanted to run to her and kiss her. He even started toward her, but Fabio caught him by his belt and pulled him back. "Where you go?" asked Fabio.

"Nowhere."

Camille called to them, "Now throw a coin."

Michael dug two coins from his pocket and handed one to Fabio.

"In your right hand," said Fabio. "Over your head. Like this." So Fabio showed him how.

"Ok," said Michael. He called to Camille, "Are you ready?"

"Ready!"

"On three," he said. Then he faced Fabio. "One, two, three!"

The men tossed their coins at the same time. Camille captured the action in her lens just as their coins flew in an arc toward the water.

Fabio and Michael turned to face the fountain. They searched for their coins, but they had already landed in the splashing water.

Fabio put his arm on Michael's shoulder. "Now you will come back to *Roma*," he said.

"Do I have a choice?" asked Michael.

"No, Michele. You do not," said Fabio.

Then a smiling Italian tourist approached Camille and said, "*Scusi.* Would you like, I take photo of all you together?" She gestured to Michael and Fabio.

"Oh, yes," said Camille. "That would be very nice. Thank you." Camille joined the men in front of the statue. She wrapped her arms around their waists. "Now behave yourselves," she said. "Both of you."

The woman snapped their picture, returned Camille's camera, nodded and waved goodbye as she left.

Camille waved back. Michael snatched her camera. "It's your turn," he said. "Now you go over there and toss your coin."

Camille opened her small purse, showed him there were no coins inside and smirked. "I told you, my darling," she said.

Michael chuckled. He dug in his pocket and planted a small coin in the palm of her left hand. He glanced at Camille's engagement ring. He couldn't remember the diamond being so big or so bright before. He let it go from his mind and shooed her away with a gentle nudge.

"I want to take this one alone," she said. She turned her back to the fountain.

"That's why I pushed you away, my pet," said Michael. "I knew you would."

Camille held the coin tightly in her hand. It was just a tiny coin that couldn't buy anything. But it was important to her because it came from Michael. She didn't want to let it go. But she knew that was foolish. So, with a sigh, she lifted her hand, and let the coin fly over her head just as he snapped the picture.

"Oh, my God!" she screamed. She turned toward the splashing water.

"What is it?" he called to her. "Oh, that was your left hand. Here. I have another coin." He dug into his pocket again.

Camille turned and faced Michael again. "No! My ring!" she cried."My ring. It's gone!"

Michael and Fabio trotted down the stone stairs."What do you mean gone?" asked Michael. He looked down at her hand, and the engagement ring was no longer there.

"It's gone," said Camille. "It must have slipped off when I threw the coin."

"Then it has to be in the fountain," said Michael. "Fabio?"

"*Si*," said Fabio. "In the fountain."

A split second later, Michael slipped off his shoes and splashed into the knee-deep water. A crowd quickly gathered. They stared in bewilderment. Camille threw off her high heels and quickly followed him in. Then Fabio. The three of them got down on their hands and knees and frantically splashed around for the ring.

"It has to be here," said Camille. "It just has to be."

"Don't worry, we'll find it," said Michael.

In their desperate search, they splashed all around in the knee-deep water. But they didn't find it. Camille wanted to scream and cry. She was ready to give up. But Michael was more determined. He told her and Fabio to keep looking.

They sprayed each other while sifting through the countless coins. Then Michael saw a sparkle bounce up at him. He knew he had spotted the ring. He quickly snatched it out of the water. But in a momentary lapse of conviction and integrity, he grappled with the thought of shoving the ring into his pocket and not saying anything. Spinning around on his knees, he saw Camille's face. She was terribly sad and desperate. Michael realized that if he held onto the ring, he would never be able to live with himself. Camille's sad eyes would haunt him forever. He stood and cried, "I've got it!"

Camille jumped up. "You do? Where?"

"Look."

She glanced down into his palm. "You did it!" she cried. "Thank you, thank you, thank you." She threw her hands around his neck and kissed him on his cheek over and over. "Oh, thank you." Then she hugged him, put her arms around his neck again and then kissed him on the lips.

Their lips parted and Michael said, "You're welcome." For a moment, their hot breath mingled in the hot air. Then he gently placed the ring on her finger. Their eyes met again. She wanted another kiss. Michael wanted more.

Fabio slapped Michael on the back. "*Bravo*, Michele," he said. "You are a hero. It is good to have you around, eh, Camilla?"

At the sound of Fabio's voice, Camille was conscious that her arms were still wrapped around Michael's neck. She quickly let go. She faced Fabio. "Yes, it is," she said. "He's a good man." Then to Michael she said, "You're a good man, Michael Valentino. I'm lucky to know you."

Michael knew he didn't have a reply that would be suitable. What could the right words be to the statement Camille had just made?

They stepped out of the fountain and onto the stone steps. Then Camille looked down at her sopping dress. She wiped at it, but that didn't help much. "What are we going to do now?" she asked.

Fabio tapped Camille on the shoulder. "Drink wine," he said.

"Drink wine?" she asked. "Are you crazy, Fabio? We're soaking wet."

"Yeah, Fabio," said Michael. "We really have to dry off and change clothes."

"No, no, no," said Fabio. "We must celebrate."

"Now?" asked Camille.

"Yes, now is the time to go to celebrate," said Fabio. "Michele has found your lost ring, and because it is now found and no longer lost, we must drink!"

"I think you've got a screw loose," said Michael.

"Well, I guess we could have a little something," said Camille.

"You're as crazy as him," said Michael.

"I am not crazy, Michele," said Fabio. "I am practical. When a great thing happens, that is the time to celebrate it. Enjoy life, Michele. That is the thing to do. *Il dolce far niente*, eh, Michele?"

"Well, you've got me there, friend," said Michael.

"I know," said Fabio.

"So where is the nearest bar?" asked Michael.

"That's the spirit, Michele," said Fabio. "It is near, just five minutes to walk."

"That sounds reasonable," said Camille. "We can dry off as we walk."

"*Perfetto*," said Fabio. "I will give you directions."

"Directions?" said Michael. "Aren't you coming? I thought you said *we* must celebrate. The three of us."

"Oh, no, Michele," said Fabio. "I cannot. I must go to work. So you and Camilla must go alone together."

"I guess we have no choice," said Michael. But deep down, he was quite glad that Fabio was going back to the hotel. Michael loved having Fabio around. He had learned so much from him about what it meant to live like an Italian, and he knew it would have been very hard to get along like he had without Fabio. But Michael also knew when enough was enough. And right now, he could think of nothing better than spending a little time alone with Camille.

"Yes, we'll be all right," said Camille. "Which way is it, Fabio?"

"Just keep going the way you are going," Fabio said. "Up these steps and keep going straight. You will see a *bella enoteca* in the fifth street. It is called Antica Enoteca. You cannot miss it."

"All right, friend," said Michael.

The three of them climbed the steps to the first street. Fabio tuned left and Michael and Camille turned right.

Fabio called to them, "Michele! Remember, just keep going the way you are going. You too Camilla. And you will not miss it!"

Michael waved to Fabio. "We got it," he said.

They turned again and started away from Fabio. "What do you think Fabio meant by that?" asked Michael.

"By what?" asked Camille.

"Just keep going the way you're going," said Michael.

"I don't know," said Camille. "They're just directions."

"Yes, but why did he say, 'You too Camille'? We're obviously going together. What did he mean?"

"I don't know, my darling," said Camille. "But maybe we'll figure it out at that *enoteca*."

Chapter Twenty-Three

CAMILLE'S FEET WERE NOW DRY. SHE STEPPED into her high heels and once again had to navigate the cobblestones. And Michael once again teased her about that. They laughed as they strolled along the five streets. Then they came to an old wine barrel in front of a bright yellow stone building and stopped. There was a large menu on an easel with the wine bar's name in gold letters. They slipped under the archway.

"My feet are dry," said Camille. "But my dress and the rest of me are still a little wet."

"So?" said Michael.

"Should we stay?" she asked. "I mean, maybe Fabio doesn't always have the answer."

"No, no, I think he does this time," said Michael. He felt his trousers. "We'll be dry soon. Let's have that drink."

"I guess you're right," said Camille. "But just one. Then it's time to go and clean up back at the hotel."

"Sure."

An approaching waiter gestured at the first table near the entrance. Michael and Camille sat and the waiter stopped at the table. "*Prego*," he said.

"All right," said Michael. "Please bring us a bottle of Chianti Classico."

"A bottle?" asked Camille.

"Sure. Why not?" said Michael.

"I thought you said we'd only stay for one drink."

"That *is* one drink," said Michael. "One bottle." He nodded to the waiter. He left.

"All right, you win," said Camille. She leaned over and picked up a strap on her shoe that had fallen down.

Michael stretched his neck and bent over to check her shoes. He chuckled. "Do you need a hand with that?" he asked.

"I've got it," said Camille. "Don't you worry about it."

Michael shook his head. "Don't you know by now that you can't maneuver with those things in Italy? There are just too many cobblestones."

"Yeah, well, I like to look nice," she said. "And high heels make my feet look nice. And they feel good too." She stared at his faded leather jacket and then leaned on his forearm. "Maybe I should give you some lessons, my sweet."

Michael stroked the worn leather. "Hey, maybe I just want to look nice too."

"For who? Fabio?" she asked.

"Oh, cut that out," said Michael.

"I know he's got a thing for you, Michael," said Camille.

"You're crazy."

Camille giggled. She smiled at Michael and said, "My darling?"

"Yes, my pet?"

"I really think we should have just one drink," said Camille. "My dress is still wet and I'm sure your clothes are too. And it is getting late."

"Well, I wouldn't worry about that," said Michael.

"If you say so," said Camille. She shrugged. *I'll humor him and then after one drink, I'll convince him to leave,* she thought.

"I don't know about you," said Michael. He stretched his arms above his head. "But I worked up an appetite splashing around in that fountain."

"You're hungry?" she asked.

"I am," he said. "And you know, we couldn't possibly finish off the whole bottle without something to eat," said Michael.

Michael called over the waiter. He arrived with the bottle of wine and poured it into the two glasses that were on the table.

Then Michael looked at Camille. "Come on, you must be starving," he said. "You're so thin."

Now why did he have to go and say that? she thought. *I hate when he does things like that. When he says the exact right thing I want to hear in a way I don't want to hear it.* "I don't know," she said. "We should get back."

Michael said, "Let's just stay till this one bottle's finished. Just this one." He put his hand over hers. "I promise."

"All right. But just this one bottle," said Camille.

"And I'll pick up the check," said Michael. He pointed his thumb at his chest.

"That's right you will," said Camille. "I never pay when I'm with a man."

Michael chuckled. Then he looked up at the waiter. Michael ordered mozzarella and pecorino cheeses, some sliced meats, sun-dried tomatoes, eggplant and cauliflower, some rustic bread and olives. The waiter left.

Michael and Camille lifted their glasses and toasted finding Camille's engagement ring in the fountain. Then they drank the first glass of the deep red wine quickly.

Because of the heat of the day, and with the tense excitement now tapering off, Michael and Camille quickly began to feel warm and fuzzy inside. Michael filled up their glasses and the second glass of wine went down even more quickly than the first.

The waiter returned with their appetizers and turned away. But Michael caught him by the arm and said, "I think it's time for another bottle." Michael lifted the bottle and shook it. "This is a special occasion."

"Really?" said Camille. "What happened to just one?"

"Oh, come on," said Michael. He picked up the bottle and shook it. "This one's nearly empty. And we can't enjoy our meal without wine." He nodded to the waiter.

"Oh, no, I'm not falling for that," said Camille. "No, sir. Not more wine. You promised. And you know what happens when you get too much wine in you."

"No. What happens?" he asked.

"You can't climb trees," said Camille. "And you can't drive a car in a little rain storm."

"Yeah, well, what about you?" said Michael. "Do I have to remind you about the garden?"

Camille reached her hand over the table and almost placed it on his cheek. Instead she pointed her finger at him and said, "You stop right there, Michael Valentino."

"Yeah. Maybe you're right," said Michael. "Maybe we should both stop now. And eat our food."

Then the second bottle of wine arrived. And Michael ordered again. Gnocci con pomodoro e basilica and spaghetti vongole. The dishes arrived quickly. They ate with gusto and sipped much more wine. And now the wine was in control. It dictated their actions. Michael and Camille were now playing a game like children. They plopped the bite-sized gnocchi into each other's mouths. Then they got more daring and tossed the gnocchi across the table hoping they'd land in each other's mouths. They laughed and delighted in the meal and the wine like long-time friends.

"Wait, wait, wait," said Camille. She lifted her purse and searched through its contents.

"What are you doing?" asked Michael. "I told you I'm going to take care of this. Now put your money away."

He reached down on his plate and picked up a sauce-smeared gnocchi. "You insult me," he said. "Now, open up."

Camille cackled, raised her head and opened her mouth. Michael gently placed the gnocchi on her tongue. She bit down softly on his fingers. Then she slowly swirled her tongue around his lingering pinky. He pulled it out very slowly, gazing over the small table at her blushing cheeks. "You've got me all flustered, my darling," said Camille. "Now I can't remember what I was doing."

With a sly grin, Michael said, "You were trying to pay."

"Oh, yes," said Camille. "I must have had a memory lapse."

"Forget about it," said Michael. "Have some more wine." He lifted the bottle, realized it was empty and then gestured to the waiter for another bottle. The Chianti was there in a flash and Michael filled their glasses.

Michael and Camille clinked their glasses together and downed the rich-bodied wine. They carried on in this way for another thirty minutes, emptying their third bottle and finally getting up to leave. By this time, everyone at Antica Enoteca was Michael's friend. He loved everybody. He waved to them all and called out his favorite Italian phrases. The patrons chuckled and played along. Then the waiter brought the bill. Michael didn't bother to look at it and handed the waiter three 100,000 lira notes. "*Basta?* Enough?" he asked.

The waiter smiled wide and nodded, He waited patiently for Michael and Camille to leave. But Michael unfolded another 100,000 lira note and handed it to him. "For you, my good man," he said. He grabbed the waiter by the shoulders and planted a kiss on both of his cheeks.

The stunned waiter and Camille laughed. Michael wrapped his arm around the man's shoulders. "Let's do it again sometime, what do you say?" he said.

The waiter handed Michael off to Camille under the arched entrance. Camille slipped under Michael's arm and they stumbled out to the narrow street. Leaning on one another, the two of them staggered through the narrow streets. They ignored the rows of old homes, restaurants, cafés and shops. And the many stares they received from the people walking along the street.

Michael pulled Camille closer. "What should we do next?" he asked.

"Go back to the hotel, of course," said Camille.

"Oh, right, right, right," said Michael. "Your hotel or mine?" He coughed a loud laugh.

"You forget, darling," said Camille. "We're staying in the same room."

"Now that's convenient," he said. "That will save us some time."

"Forget it, my sweet," said Camille. "We're not doing anything like that." But as red surrounds white on a barber shop pole, they were tied to one another. To the laughing onlookers, they were merely another drunken couple in love. Entangled and in love.

"Ah, you're too drunk anyway," said Michael. "It wouldn't be any fun."

"You're the one who's drunk," said Camille. "And crazy."

"That's right," he said. "You're not drunk. Just crazy. Crazy not to be crazy about me. Like I am about you, my pet." He gazed at her smiling eyes.

"Oh, I know, I know," said Camille. "You're right about me, my darling. And I know how you feel." But in her heart, she thought, *I am crazy about him. I wish I could tell him.*

Michael leaned on her heavily. "Let's go home," he said. "Wherever that is."

"All right," said Camille.

"No. Wait," he said. "I just remembered. I have to stop at a tobacco shop."

"But you don't smoke," she said.

"I know."

Camille looked at the buildings along both sides of the street. There was a small *tabaccheria* on the right side about twenty feet away. They staggered inside. The owner was a short man with thick silver hair and beard. "*Prego,*" he said.

Michael looked at Camille and laughed.

"What was that for?" she asked.

"He's funny," said Michael. "I love his funny voice."

Camille faced the man. "Don't pay any attention to him," she said. "He's drunk."

"Do not worry, *signorina,*" said the man. "I see many like him every day."

Now Camille laughed. And Michael laughed along with her.

"What do you want?" the man asked them.

Camille shrugged. "I don't know," she said. She faced Michael. "What do you want, darling?"

"Cigarettes," said Michael. "Whatever kind you have. It doesn't matter."

"Okay," said the man. *"Ecco."* He handed Michael a package of Italian cigarettes. *"Trecento mila."*

Michael took a bill from his pocket and handed it to the man. "You keep the change, good sir," he said.

"Grazie," said the man.

Michael fingered the pack of cigarettes. He suddenly looked depressed and he sighed. "Maybe I should take up smoking," he said.

"Let me see those," said Camille.

Michael handed her the cigarette package. Camille took a half-moment to look it over.

"Maybe you're right," said Camille.

"What? Why?"

"Look what it says here," said Camille. She held the package so Michael could read it.

"It says these cigarettes are like love," said Michael.

"Right," said Camille. "Isn't that a hoot? This country is really all about love, isn't it? Even its cigarettes are in love."

"At least somebody admits it," said Michael.

"Darling, what are you driving at?" asked Camille.

"Oh, nothing at all," said Michael. "But maybe I *should* start smoking. It might help me forget about my half-brother."

"No, it won't," said Camille. "And anyway, why would you want to forget?"

"It's over," he said. "That's why."

"It's not over till it's over," said Camille. "So don't quit. Not yet."

"You don't know," said Michael. "It's over."

"We'll find him," said Camille. "We will. Just a little longer. Have faith. And we will find him."

The owner had watched Camille and Michael as their conversation went back and forth. "Find who?" asked the man.

Camille said, "Were looking for his half-brother. We're from New York. And Michael here has a half-brother somewhere in Rome. That's why we came here. To find his Italian half-brother."

"What's his name?" asked the shop owner.

"I don't know," said Michael. "What's the difference?"

"Then what is his family name?" asked the owner.

"Same as mine," said Michael. "Valentino."

"Valentino?" asked the man.

"Yes. That's what I said," said Michael. "Valentino."

"I know Valentino," said the man.

"What?" Michael almost reached his hand across the shop's counter. He wanted to draw the owner closer. "Did you say you know a Valentino?"

"I know a woman. Signora Valentino," said the shop owner. "She come here all the time."

"And how old is she?" asked Michael.

"*Cinquant'anni.* Fifty years about," said the man. "She has black hair and dark eyes. Like you."

"Like me?" asked Michael.

The man looked closer at Michael's face. He nodded. "*Sì.* Like you. Maybe she have a son. I don't know."

Michael turned to Camille. "Did you hear that, Camille? She's fifty and her name is Valentino."

"I heard. I heard," said Camille. She faced the man. "What's her first name?"

The man lifted his head slightly. "Caterina," he said.

"Caterina!" cried Michael. "It must be her!"

"Yes, it could be," said Camille.

Camille stared at the owner. "So where do we find this woman by the name of Caterina Valentino?" she asked.

"I write her address," said the shop owner. He opened a small notebook and wrote down the address. He tore the paper from the notebook and handed it to Michael. "*Ecco. Via Borgognona settanta,*" said the man. "Not far. You find easy."

"That's great!" said Michael. "This is great! Incredible! I can't believe my luck."

Michael shook the shop owner's hand. "*Grazie,* my friend, *grazie,*" he said.

"*Prego,*" replied the man.

Michael turned away and started out of the shop. "I really can't believe my luck," he said. He stared down at the address on the piece of paper.

"Yes," said Camille. She followed Michael out of the tobacco shop. "What are the odds?"

Chapter Twenty-Four

IT WAS QUIET AT THE HOTEL THE NEXT morning. The heat was stifling and the guests did not venture out of their air-conditioned rooms. Cecilia was behind the front desk filing her nails while Patrizia was doodling a cartoon rabbit on a yellow writing pad. Fabio spun himself wildly in the revolving door and raced into the lobby. Fifteen minutes late and not dressed up to the hotel's standards, with his shirt tails out of his tight, black trousers, Fabio stopped short on the opposite side of the counter. "We have to do more about Michele and Camilla," he said. He was panting as he tucked in his shirt.

Cecilia looked at him with eyes squinting. "What more?"she asked. "Have you thought of it?"

"I do not know," said Fabio. "Just more. Poor, poor Michele."

Glancing up from her doodle, Patrizia asked, "Why poor?"

"Michele is in deep, deep love," said Fabio. He stared at the two women. "Deep, deep. And it is a bad case of the deep, deep love. We were out with him last night. Fiorella was flirting with him a lot, but he did not have eyes for her. Instead, his eyes were reserved for the one."

"Who?" said Patrizia. "Who is the one?"

Cecilia stopped filing her nails. She raised her head and said, "I know exactly who is the one."

"Who?" said Patrizia, her nostrils twitching.

"Is it not obvious?" said Cecilia.

Patrizia shook her head. "Not to me."

Cecilia grinned. "Camilla, of course," she said. "He loves the girl staying in the same room. She is Michele's one."

"Really?"

Fabio adjusted his belt. "Of course," he said. "I have known it the whole time, since they checked in yesterday."

"You have known?" said Patrizia.

Fabio chuckled. "Who do you think joked to them that we had only one room left?"

Cecilia shook her head with a small laugh. She wiggled her index finger in the air and pointed at her chest. "But who do you think was it who convinced them to do it?" she said.

Fabio nodded, glanced from Cecilia to Patrizia, and said, "We must do more."

Just then, Camille and Michael were walking briskly down the stairs. They passed by the front desk with big smiles and a cheery "*Buongiorno*".

The three employees followed them with their eyes.

"They don't look like they need more to me," said Patrizia.

Camille and Fabio stared on. Michael and Camille waved goodbye as then exited the hotel. They turned right out of the hotel and headed west, passing the arcade of flowers at Campo de' Fiori. It was only ten o'clock and the sky's sun was beating down hard on the pavement through the deep blue sky. Michael and Camille began to break a sweat almost immediately. "What do you think they were staring at?" asked Cecilia.

"I don't know," said Michael. "Fabio was the one who gave me the directions to the house."

"Did you tell him whose house it was?"

"No way," said Michael. "I want to surprise him. I told him it was an art gallery."

"Fabio works at the hotel and this is his city," said Camille. "Don't you think he's going to know it's not an art gallery?"

"Come on," said Michael. "It's Fabio."

"You're right. How silly of me," said Camille. "You are right more times than I give you credit for, my darling."

"How nice of you to notice, my pet," said Michael. "Once we meet my half- brother and her mother, and I am sure it's them, then we'll surprise him and Cecilia with the good news."

"And then we'll go out and celebrate," said Camille. "That would certainly be something to declare."

"Certainly."

"I still can't believe you got that great tip from the shop owner," said Camille.

"I know," said Michael. "Who would have thought he knew Caterina Valentino? And her address. What a stroke of luck."

Two large dragonflies buzzed in a nearby hazelnut tree, and a carpenter bee dove menacingly at them, but then flew past. Michael and Camille gazed up on a small, single-family home with a dark red roof that needed patching. It was a very old house with grey-brown stone walls. Michael eyed the splintered front door. He didn't see a door bell, so he pounded on the door. Hopping up and down like a jackrabbit, he said, "This is it. I can feel it."

"Yes, very exciting," said Camille. "What do you think he looks like?"

"I don't know," said Michael. "Sort of like me. But I bet he's short." His words came quickly, pacing out his anxiety to get inside.

There was no activity behind the door, so Michael pounded harder on the door. One minute later, a man of about seventy with a sunburned bald head and grey-white beard swung it open. *"Si?"* he said.

"Buongiorno. My name is Michael Valentino," said Michael. "And this is Camille. We've come a long way, from New York."

But the older man did not say anything. He just stood there, holding onto the door, and staring at them.

Michael turned to Camille and said, "I wish I could speak better Italian."

"Just try," she said.

Michael faced the man. "*Mi chiamo Michele Valentio, di New York,*" he said Michael. "*Sei il Signor Valentino?*"

"*Si, Valentino. Si,*" said the man.

"I think it might be Caterina's father," said Camille.

"Right," said Michael. "Do you have a daughter?" he asked the man.

The old man stared at Michael, but didn't answer.

"*Una figlia. Hai una figlia?*" asked Michael.

"*Si, una figlia bella,*" said the man. "Caterina."

"*Io sono anche Valentino,*" said Michael. "And I…*e conosco tua figlia.*"

Camille tugged on Michael's sleeve. "Tell him you know his daughter."

Michael said, "I just did."

"We came to meet her," said Camille.

Then the old man grabbed Michael by his arms and pulled him inside. He indicated to Camille to follow. Then he ushered them through a dark narrow hallway that curved slightly up to the dining room. The picture-less walls were a dingy yellow. Camille grimaced at the large spider's web in the corner near the peeling ceiling.

The old man sat them down on worn wooden chairs. Their edges had been smoothed down into soft rounds over the years. Five empty bowls and plates and a basket of home-made bread had been set around a dried-up bouquet of small wildflowers. Mr. Valentino moved around the table to an old cabinet, bent down and pulled from it a cheap bottle of red table wine.

"Celebration!" cried the old man. He reached into the china closet and pulled out three wine glasses and poured. "Drink. You are *famiglia*," he said, whacking them both on their backs. He turned toward the kitchen. "Maria!" he bellowed. "Bring two more plates and bowls. We have guests!"

Michael wondered about this miracle of language. He turned to Camille and said, "He speaks English."

Camille's eyes went wide. "Apparently," she said.

A chubby little old woman scurried through the arched doorway from the kitchen, carrying two bowls and plates balanced on top of a large pot of minestrone soup. "*Buongiorno*," she said. "I am Maria Valentino." Her husband lifted the plates and she set the old pot down on the table. "Welcome to my home." She didn't even question who these two new guests were. If they were good enough for her husband, they were good enough for her.

Mr. Valentino told his wife that Michael and Camille had come from New York to meet them. And Maria wrapped her chubby arms around him. Then she did the same with Camille. "Sit, sit. *Mangia, mangia*," she ordered.

Mr. Valentino pulled two more glasses from the china closet and poured wine for his wife and the visitors. They were just about to toast their good fortune when another woman entered through the front door. She was in her early fifties. There were a few wrinkles around her eyes but her hair was still a shiny black. And she carried herself with confidence. A man of about fifty-five and a younger woman followed the first woman inside.

"Ah, Caterina, Paolo. Annabella. *Bene*. Come, meet our new family," said Mr. Valentino. He waved them in with his chunky hand.

All sat down at the table together. They clinked wine glasses and there were shouts of *"Salute!"* Then Michael told the story of how he and Camille had learned of the Valentinos from the shop owner. After words of congratulation and some mention of *"fortuna"*, they began slurping up a steaming bean soup. Mrs. Valentino ran back to the kitchen and returned with a large antipasti platter loaded with dry salame, prosciutto di Parma, sopressata, mortadella, mozzarella and parmigiano reggiano. The center was filled with some fried calamari rings, anchovies smothered in olive oil and assorted olives.

Mrs. Valentino set three large serving forks in the platter and said, *"Prego."*

Michael leaned over to Camille. "She kind of reminds me of my mother."

"Why wouldn't she?" said Camille. "She's Italian, my sweet."

Mr. Valentino ignored the appetizers. He drained his cup of wine instantly and refilled all the glasses on the table, whether they needed to be filled or not. "Drink up! Drink up! Do not be shy. We have many more wine," he said. He was in an especially good mood.

"I am a very lucky man," said Mr. Valentino. "To be surrounded by *la mia famiglia*. There is no better thing in life, eh, Michele?

"I think so, too," said Michael. "That's why I came looking for my half-brother." He glanced at Caterina. "And his mother."

Caterina smiled back at Michael. Then she realized something. "Did you say half-brother?"

"Yes. It all started with my father," said Michael. "When he died, I found his letters and photographs. They led me to all of you." Up until that moment, Michael hadn't realized just how much he had missed his father. He knew he had found something important when he found his father's personal belongings. But he didn't realize how strong his own father-son bond really was. "And now I have found all of you."

Michael raised his glass to make a toast. Mr. Valentino followed and then the rest. Except Caterina. "Here's to—" began Michael.

"Michele, you have a half-brother in Italy?" asked Caterina.

"Of course," said Michael. "Your son." Michael looked around the room. "When does he get here?"

Caterina shook her head. "Michele, I have no son," she said. "Only one daughter."

Everyone lowered their glasses.

"But how could that be?" asked Michael.

"Wait a minute," said Camille. She turned to Michael. "You have the photos, right?"

"Sure."

"Well, my darling, just show Caterina the photos," said Camille. "That'll clear up everything."

So Michael pulled from his jacket pocket three of the old photos he had found in his mother's attic in New York. He passed them to Caterina first. Pointing to the young lady with the big belly, he said, "Isn't this you?"

Caterina shook her head. "No, that is not me," she said.

"So, you don't have a son?" asked Michael.

"I have one daughter," said Caterina. "She is here. You already met her. Annabella."

Michael let out a large breath. "Whoa," he said, almost in a whisper. "I guess I've made a big mistake."

Caterina looked at Michael with empathy. "I am so sorry, Michele," she said.

"Yeah. Me too," said Michael. A heavy silence filled the room for a long moment. "I guess we should be going then." Michael stood and looked at Camille.

She nodded and stood beside him.

"Thank you for the meal," said Michael. He raised a hand over to Mr. Valentino. "And the wine." He paused only a moment as the others rose. But they said nothing.

Michael turned and walked away.

"We're sorry we troubled you," said Camille.

Michael did not turn back. He quickly passed through the front door with Camille trailing closely behind.

With a deadpanned expression and not a single word, Michael started away from the house with its peeling paint. All he could think about was getting as far away from that house as possible. Camille placed a hand on his shoulder and said, "It's all right, Michael. We *will* find him. There is still time."

Michael replied with nothing more than a single nod and a heavy sigh.

"I think we need a drink," said Camille.

They wandered along the cobblestoned streets, not saying anything at all, until they came to Piazza Navona, a large square brimming with ancient history and modern activity. A sea of visitors flocked to Bernini's immense Fountain of Four Rivers, with its soaring Egyptian obelisk in the center of the river gods who had been frozen forever in majestic poses. There were street performers juggling their colorful balls and tossing their bodies about like they were made of rubber. Families were gathering at cafés, and milling tourists were searching for a piece of Roman history. Amateur artists also dotted the piazza. Canvases ripe with brilliant reds and golds and blues abounded, some capturing the beauty of the rolling hills of nearby Tuscany, and others the winding, home-studded cliffs of the stunning Amalfi Coast.

But Michael and Camille were focused only on their disappointment of visiting the wrong house. They strolled inside Tre Scalini, an iconic café. A rich scent of dark espresso wafted about the bar.

"Maybe a coffee instead of wine," said Michael.

"I know what's even better than *that*," said Camille.

"What?"

"How about coffee gelato?" she said.

"Perfect."

So Michael ordered two coffee gelatos. He paid and handed one to Camille. "It's too nice to sit inside," he said.

"Won't we be too hot in the sun?" asked Camille.

"We'll manage," he said. "Come on."

They found a seat on one of the stone benches outside. Michael instantly jumped up and started pacing in front of her. "I'll tell you," he said. "What a waste of time."

Camille dug into her gelato with the tiny, plastic spoon. Thrusting her tongue like a snake she said, "What's the matter? Don't you like it, my darling?"

"Sure I do," said Michael. "I'm waiting for it to melt and drip down my hand." He started pacing again. "I mean, why do I even bother? I'm never going to find him. How could I have been so stupid to think his last name would be the same as mine?"

"It was a perfectly justifiable mistake. Anyone could have made it," said Camille. "And as for my gelato, I want to roll around in it, it's so good." She bent her head to the side and licked around her cone.

He stopped pacing and looked at her. "I guess you're right. But I don't know about the rolling around," said Michael. He twisted the cone while licking the gelato. "But it is good. Better than ice cream."

Camille finished the gelato and crunched on the last bits of her cone. Then she ran her tongue provocatively along the contours of her lips.

Michael calmed down and sat next to her.

A pair of youngsters jumped up from a nearby bench and splashed in the fountain. Their young mothers proudly watched with protective eyes. They flitted about the piazza like two beautiful butterflies dancing in a tree branch.

Camille clutched her blouse. "I wish I had my camera. Those two little girls dancing in the fountain would have made a precious picture."

"Yeah. Why *didn't* you bring your camera today?" asked Michael. "I thought you would have wanted to take pictures at the...well. It was the wrong house and the wrong family anyway, so."

"What are you thinking about, my pet" asked Camille. "I mean right now."

"I don't know," said Michael. "Nothing."

"Nothing?"

"What do you think I'm thinking about?" he said. "That I'm never going to find my half-brother."

"That's old already," said Camille. "Come on. You're being ridiculous. You want to know what I'm thinking right now?"

"Not really."

"Well, I'm going to tell you anyway," said Camille. "I'm thinking that we should follow that delicious gelato with a glass of wine."

"Again with the wine?" asked Michael.

But Camille ignored his question and said, "Hey, you got that worthless tip from the owner of a tobacco shop."

"Yeah."

"And you bought a pack of cigarettes there."

"So."

"So, you don't smoke."

Michael pulled the cigarettes from his pocket. "For Fabio," he said.

"Figures," said Camille.

Michael fingered the package and said, "And I forgot to give them to him."

"You've gotten pretty close to Fabio, haven't you, my sweet?" asked Camille.

"Well…yeah."

"Sure you have."

"Well, he's done so much for me. For us," said Michael. He gazed on Camille. "He's been like a…"

"Brother to you?"

"Well, yeah, I guess he has."

Camille smiled and nodded.

"Wait a minute," said Michael. "You don't think Fabio is…"

"Why not? He could be," said Camille. "What if all that stuff his friends said about him last night was true?"

"Nah," said Michael. "It's just not possible, like Fabio said."

"But why not?" asked Camille. "He *is* the right age. And he really does look like you."

"You think?"

"Of course," said Camille. "And he cares about you like a brother would. Right?"

"He does," said Michael. "And whenever I tell him I've lost all hope in finding my half-brother, he always says, 'Don't worry, Michele. We'll find him. I promise you.' But he never does anything about it. It's like he's intentionally avoiding the topic."

In that moment, Michael and Camille watched Fabio race across the square. He stopped in front of them. Fabio was panting and sweating. "Michele, I am so glad I have found you," he said. "I came to the piazza to find you and to tell you, and you are here."

"I'm here," said Michael. "So is Camille."

"*Si. Ciao,* Camilla," he said.

Camille glanced up at him and said, "*Ciao, Fabio.*"

"How did you know we were here?" asked Michael.

"When foreigners cannot find their family, this is where they come," said Fabio.

"That's not funny, Fabio," said Michael.

"I am sorry, Michele."

"It's okay. Forget it." Michael put his hand on Fabio's arm. "So, Fabio, what did you want?"

"I came to find you, because I have something I must confess," said Fabio.

And then, they both blurted it out at the same time.

"It's me!" said Fabio.

"It's you!" said Michael.

Camille smiled. "I was right," she said.

"*Si*, you were right," said Fabio. "He is me. I am he. Fabio. Your brother."

Michael stared him down. "If it's true, Fabio," he said, "if you're my half-brother, then why didn't you tell me before?"

"You were not ready," said Fabio. He gently put his hand on Michael's shoulder.

Michael wrenched his shoulder away from Fabio. "*I* wasn't ready?" he asked.

"*Sì.* You."

"And just how long have you known?" asked Michael. "Since the game at the club last night?"

"No. I have known since you checked in to the hotel," said Fabio.

"And you never told me?" said Michael. "This is unbelievable! We could have saved so much time and energy. I was searching for someone who was right in front of me."

"It was necessary," said Fabio. "I had to check your loyalty."

"What are you talking about?" asked Michael.

Camille then added, "Yes, it's confusing to me too, Fabio. What exactly do you mean?"

"Well, if I told Michele I was his half-brother, then I would not have known him truly," said Fabio. He faced Michael. "And you would not know me."

"What the hell does that mean?" asked Michael.

Fabio looked into Michael's eyes. "It took time for me to know if you were my half-brother because you wanted a half-brother or because you wanted me," he said.

"What?"

"It is the truth," said Fabio. "How could I know what kind of man you were? I needed to spend time with you. I needed to know you, Michele."

"So you were just testing me?" said Michael.

"Something like that," said Fabio. "And you passed."

"Is that supposed to cheer me up?" said Michael.

"*Sì.*"

"Well, it doesn't," said Michael. "In fact, it makes me realize just how much of a liar you are. You withheld the one piece of information that you knew was the most important thing in the world to me."

"I did not lie," said Fabio.

"You tricked me," said Michael. "And not in a good way."

"I am sorry, Michele," said Fabio. "But it was the only way I knew. It was *my* way. I had to know."

Michael pushed the air between him and Fabio. "I don't want this. I can't deal with this right now," he said. He started to walk away.

Camille started after him. She grabbed onto his arm. "Wait!" she said.

"What?" Michael panted. "I have to get out of here."

"Wait," she said again. "We should give Fabio a chance to explain."

"*We?*" asked Michael.

"Well, yeah," said Camille. "This almost means as much to me as it does to you. I've been with you from the beginning. You know that."

"Yes, well…"

"Well what?" she asked.

"Maybe it's time to end it then," said Michael.

"Michael, you're being unreasonable," said Camille. "And childish. All Fabio did was take a little time to get to know you. He wanted to see if you were really who you said you were."

"Why couldn't he have just said that?" asked Michael. He would not look at Fabio.

"Well, how did he know?" said Camille. "You could have made it all up."

"Si," said Fabio. He took a step closer to them.

"Made it up?' said Michael. "Who would make up a story like that?"

"It's possible," said Camille.

"*Si*," Fabio said again.

"That's crazy," said Michael. "Why would I come all the way to Italy, with proof—the pictures, the letters—if it weren't true?"

"Who knows?" said Camille. "But it is possible. Fabio was just making sure. He had a lot on the line?"

"What do you mean?" asked Michael.

Camille glanced over at Fabio. He wore a hopeful smile. Then she looked back at Michael. "If you weren't really his half-brother," she said, "but maybe somebody who was trying to pull something or use him for who knows what, then he would have been tremendously hurt."

"*Si, si*," said Fabio. He took one more step toward them.

Michael glanced at Fabio and then looked back at Camille. Hesitating, he said, "I didn't think of that."

"You see?" said Camille.

Michael turned back for another glance at Fabio. But he spoke to Camille again. "I was so focused on me finding my half-brother and how I would feel that I never even thought about how it would affect him."

"Now you get it," said Camille. "And even though Fabio was feeling you out, he was always there for you."

"That's true," said Michael. "I just wish I had known that when we were doing all those things together. We could have been doing them as brothers."

Fabio took another step closer and placed his hand on Michael's back. "We were," he said.

Michael turned around and saw a tear on Fabio's cheek. "I'm sorry, Fabio," he said. "I shouldn't have gotten angry with you."

"It is all right, Michele," said Fabio. He turned Michael so he completely faced him and then drew him into a strong embrace.

Camille closed her arms around her chest. She smiled at the two men as they hugged. "Yes, I really believe it is," she said.

After their hug, Michael looked at Fabio. "Wait a minute. Fabio, what made you change your mind about me?" he asked. "What's different now than when we first met? What happened?"

"Last night," said Fabio.

"What about last night?" asked Michael.

"You did not leave the club with Fiorella," said Fabio.

"So? I didn't feel anything for her."

"*Si*," said Fabio. "You left with Camilla." He looked at her with a hopeful smile.

"That's right. You did," said Camille. Then she said rather quickly, "Ooh. I have an idea."

Michael and Fabio both asked, "What?"

"Let's celebrate!"

"*Si*. Great idea, Camilla," said Fabio. "And I know just the place."

Chapter Twenty-Five

FABIO STEPPED OUT OF THE TAXI FIRST. Then he helped Michael and finally Camille out. He fidgeted in place in front of a small tan house. It was two stories with windows that were close together. There was a small white fence off to one side that enclosed a garden where some tomato plants and some basil was growing. Fabio looked up at the windows and then pulled on his collar. "Michele, she is going to love you," he said. "You too, Camilla."

Camille smiled at him. She primped the small bow of her pale pink dress. "And we're going to love her too," she said. "Right, my sweet?"

"Of course we are," said Michael.

Fabio rang the doorbell. Then he put a key in the lock and opened the front door.

"Why'd you ring the bell if you had the key?" asked Camille.

"To alert her," said Fabio. He looked at Camille. "I want her to be ready for Michele. He can be so scary."

"You are funny, Fabio," said Michel.

They passed through the doorway and climbed two steps into the foyer. A woman was waiting near a small table with a vase holding a bunch of wild flowers. She had hair that was a deep raven color with only a few white strands. Her arms were folded and she was tapping her foot. "Where have you been?" she said.

Fabio looked down at his wrist. He wasn't wearing a watch. "Eh," he said. "I am Fabio."

"I know who you are," said the woman. "Come here and give Mama a kiss."

Fabio rushed to her and kissed her on both cheeks. Then they hugged. Michael's eyes went wide. His mouth hung open for a moment. Then he said, "Caterina?"

Fabio's mother released her son and walked over to Michael. "Michele," she said, more sure than he was about her. She pulled him in for a hug.

Fabio pressed his hand to his heart. A large feeling of re-lief washed over him. He glanced over at Camille who was welling up.

"It is all right to cry," he said. "In *Italia*, we cry very much. But only for happy things."

Caterina released Michael, kissed him on both cheeks and then gazed at Camille. "And Camilla," she said. Then the two women also kissed and hugged.

Caterina then ushered them into the dining room. She glanced at Michael. "I was so happy when Fabio told me you were coming to see me for dinner. It is the happiest time of day," she said.

"I like it very much too," said Michael.

Then Caterina asked them all to sit and the meal commenced right away.

Appetizers and pasta came out of the kitchen together. Fabio with wide eyes rubbed his hands together. It was a mouth-watering display of mozzarella and parmigiano cheese, assorted sliced meats, sun-dried tomatoes, eggplant and cauliflower, and of course loaves of rustic bread and olives.

Camille leaned in close to Michael and said, "Look at this spread. I guess Italian mothers are all the same."

"Is that bad?" asked Michael.

"Just the opposite," said Camille. "I think it's wonderful." She leaned in closer to him and tapped her shoulder against his.

The pasta dishes were a gnocci con pomodoro e basilica and a rigatoni all' amatriciana. The memory of Angelina's amatriciana teased both Michael's and Camille's minds. Fabio opened the wine. It was a red wine from Rome, light and palatable. Fabio filled four glasses and indicated he was ready to make a toast.

"There are no words, in English or in *Italiano* that I can say to tell you what I feel," he said. "My brother Michele has found me and I have found you." He pressed his hand against his chest. "It is more than my heart can bear." He looked Michael in the eyes. *"Mio fratello."*

They clicked glasses and then Caterina and Camille clapped and cheered like they were watching an Italian opera.

As they began eating, the conversation was light and happy with nods of appreciation and smiles of delight over the tasty food. Then Caterina turned to Michael and asked, "Michele, how did you know you had a half-brother?"

"Fabio didn't tell you?" asked Michael.

"*Sì,* he told me," said Caterina. "But not all. I would like to hear from your lips." She smiled at him and rested her chin on her fist.

"Well," said Michael. "It all started the day of my father's funeral. After my family and I arrived home, I went up in the attic of the old house and found some of Dad's things. There was his uniform from the war and some letters he wrote to his parents and photographs from his time in Italy. You know, in Naples."

"*Certo,*" said Caterina. "Of course. *Napoli*, where I was born."

"Me too," said Fabio.

"Of course," said Michael. His eyes scanned the others at the table, but they didn't say anything.

"So, when I found the photographs," Michael continued, "I realized that Dad had had a relationship with a beautiful young lady in Naples." He looked at Caterina and she smiled at him. "And she was pregnant."

"With me," said Fabio. "That was me in her big belly."

"Yes, that was you, Fabio," said Michael. "Well, when I questioned my mother about it, she had no choice but to tell me the truth."

"And what did she say, Michele?" asked Caterina.

"She told me all that she knew," said Michael. "That my father did have a relationship in Italy, but it was before he ever met my mother. She told me that he had met a lovely young lady, not much more than a girl, and that she was carrying his baby. But he had left Italy before that baby was born because the war had ended and he had to come home to America."

"Is that all?" asked Caterina.

"And that the young lady was kind and pretty and very much in love."

"How could she know that?" asked Fabio.

"My mother said that she could see it in the photographs," said Michael. "And in my father's eyes."

"Really?" asked Camille.

"Yes," said Michael. "She said that they only talked about Caterina once, but it was enough to know that he really loved her too."

A tear fell down Caterina's cheek. She reached her hand over the table and gently placed it on top of Michael's.

"But why, then did he leave?" asked Camille.

"My mother didn't say," said Michael. "She told me that she didn't feel it was her place to ask my father. And that she felt so lucky that he loved my mother too."

Fabio looked at his mother. "Can you tell us why he left?" he asked.

"*Mi dispiace*," she said. "I am sorry, Fabio, but I can't. He was your father and I know you want to know about him. But a woman's heart is different than a man's. Some things she cannot say."

Fabio now reached over and rested his hand on Caterina's. "I understand," he said.

There was a silent moment. But soon enough, Caterina broke that silence. "So, what about you and Camilla, Michele?"

Michael sipped at his wine. "What do you mean?" he asked.

"You are together, no?" she asked.

Michael waved a hand. "No, no. Not together," he said. "We met in Naples, when I was looking for Fabio. It was all by accident."

"Accident?" she said. "Or was it destiny?"

Michael chuckled. "I've never been that big on destiny," he said. "There's too much on the line to allow destiny to run your life."

"Oh, I don't know if it means running your life," said Camille. "We found Fabio. That was destiny, I would say. But your life has more elements than only destiny."

"Who knows?" said Michel. "Maybe you're right. Maybe destiny does exist and in some small way it plays a part. Maybe it's destiny and luck and perseverance all rolled up into one. All I know is that if I hadn't found my dad's stuff, I wouldn't be here now."

Fabio and Caterina smiled at each other.

Michael suddenly stood and picked up his glass of wine. "I'd like to make a toast now, if that's all right," he said. His eyes glanced around at the others at the table.

Caterina and Camille nodded. Fabio said, *"Prego."*

"A few months ago, I found a box in the attic of my mother's house," Michael began. "Back then, I had no idea how my life would change. I knew nothing of what would become of me, of who I would meet, or what I would see. Not even what I would eat." He glanced down at the *amatriciana* dish in front of him, then over at Camille. He acknowledged her smile and continued. "Or drink." He smiled back at her, recalling the wine they had shared on their journey from Naples to Rome. "It took me months to prepare for my trip. I studied your language and your customs. I read maps of Italy and made reservations and appointments. And although I was born into an Italian family in New York, I knew nothing of what it meant to be Italian. I had hoped I would be prepared once I got here. But do you know what happened?" He glanced around but the others sat quietly. "Nothing. I still knew nothing once I got to Italy. It was like I was a baby, just born into the world and not ready for any of it. Like a baby, I was curious about the world. I had many, many questions and desires. And I had no idea where I would get the answers to all my questions. It turned out that you Fabio and you Camille would help me find my way. Because of you two, I could now navigate this new world. If I hadn't met you two, I would have surely failed at this new life in Italy. I would have been nothing to no one and all of my efforts would have been in vain. Here, in Italy is where I was re-born. And I couldn't have been without you. I am so blessed that I have found both of you." Michael glanced at Caterina. "And you Caterina." She blew him a kiss. "I have become a new man because of my journey to Italy. It's amazing what we can do when we try, and we have others who help. What I could not do in New York in months I have accomplished here in just days. So here's to Fabio and Camille." Michael raised his glass. "My new best brother and my new best friend." He glanced at Caterina. "And my new best half-mother."

The others raised their glasses.

"Here, here!" said Camille.

"Salute!" cried Fabio and Caterina.

There was some clapping. Then Michael sat and they resumed the meal. Glad sounds circled the table as they delighted in their pasta dishes. Fabio told the story of how his friends had played that what if game at the club where they had imagined Fabio was Michael's half-brother. All at the table had a hearty laugh. Especially Fabio.

Then Caterina began piling up the plates. She looked at Michael. "Where do you go next?" she asked.

"I guess I go home," he said. "Back to New York."

"Bene," said Caterina. "And you Camilla?"

"Well…" Camille said.

Michael caught her hesitation before the others. "Camille's heading to Paris next," he said very quickly. "To get married."

"Is that true?" asked Caterina.

"Yes, it is," said Camille. "Claude my fiancé is waiting for me there."

"I see," said Caterina.

"I don't like Paris," said Fabio. "It is too…I don't know. Just too."

"Really?" asked Camille.

Caterina glanced at Michael. He wore a glowering face.

"*Si*. You should not go there, Camilla," said Fabio. "It is just too…you know. You do not belong there."

Camille chuckled. "You *are* funny, Fabio," she said.

"I am serious, Camilla," said Fabio.

Caterina again looked at Michael. She waited for him to protest, but he sat in silence. His angry face was enough for her to know what was on his mind.

Camille shook her head and stood. "I'll help you clear the table," she said to Caterina.

"It is all right, Camilla," said Caterina. "I can manage."

Michael looked at Camille. "You're not going," he said.

"What did you say?" said Camille.

"I said you're not going to Paris."

"I think I am," said Camille.

"You're not."

"I am," said Camille. She put her hands on her hips.

"You're not."

"I am," he said again.

Fabio stood next. "See, even Michele agrees," he said. "Camilla, really, you should not go."

"Fabio, that is enough," said Caterina. She grabbed his arm lightly. "Camilla is a woman. She is old enough to make up her mind."

"But—"

"No but, Fabio," said Caterina. "In fact, why don't you go out to the garden, Camilla? You and Michele. It is a very nice night."

"The garden?" asked Camille.

"She means the back yard," said Fabio. "But Mama, I don't think—"

"*Basta!* Enough," said Caterina. "I think Michele and Camilla need a little privacy."

"The back yard?" asked Michael.

"*Sì*. It is a very lovely night," said Caterina. "Fabio will show you."

"Come," said Fabio. "I will show you how to get there."

"All right," said Camille.

She followed Fabio through the dining room to a porch that led down a small flight of stairs. "Down here," said Fabio. "There is your lovely night."

Fabio looked behind Camille, but Michael wasn't there. "Where is Michele?" he asked.

"I don't know," said Camille. "I thought he was right behind me."

"I go look for him," said Fabio. "You wait here. With your lovely night."

Then Fabio ran back to the dining room. He saw Michael snooping around. His movements were quick. He picked up a bottle of wine and was looking at the label. Caterina was already in the kitchen washing the dishes. "Michele, what happened?" asked Fabio. "What are you doing?"

"Do you have any wine from Chianti?" asked Michael. He put the bottle that was in his hand down.

"*Si. Certo,*" said Fabio. "But why?"

"I need a bottle," said Michael.

"*Si,*" said Fabio. He searched a cabinet and chose a dark bottle. "*Ecco.* Chianti Classico. The best."

"Perfect," said Michael. "He worked the corkscrew fast and there was a small pop."

Then Michael raced to the kitchen. He said, "Excuse me," to Caterina at the sink, and started pouring the wine down the sink.

"What are you doing?" asked Fabio.

Michael stopped pouring when the bottle was half full. "Saving myself," he said. Then he dashed out of the kitchen and onto the back porch and then down the stairs.

Michael stopped a few steps away from Camille. She was sitting on a stone bench facing him. Her eyes sparkled in the bright moonlight. And her smirk was all he needed to assure him that what he was about to say would not be in vain.

He took one very slow step towards her. "You know, this moonlight reminds me of something," he said.

"Oh, yeah? What's that?" she asked.

"I think you know."

"Montesole?"

"Bingo," said Michael.

Camille chuckled. "And that bottle reminds *me* of something."

"And what's that?" asked Michael.

"I think *you* know."

"I know," he said. He took one more slow step towards her. "The bench looks similar too."

She spun her head around. "It does, doesn't it?"

"And I have a slight recollection of a couple of hazelnut trees in that garden," he said.

"There were trees," said Camille. "But not hazelnut ones. They were cedars and elms."

"How could you remember that?" asked Michael. "You were stinking drunk."

"I've never been," she said. "A lady never gets stinking anything, my darling."

"Right. Not drunk," said Michael. "And I think what you said went something like, 'I had a little wine, and the moon, and then you're going to think I forgot. And then remind me of how very charming you are.' I was pretty charming, wasn't I?"

Camille smirked and there was a small chuckle too.

"And you said something else. Something about the full moon and the bright starry sky. Then you accused me of trickery. You thought I thought you forgot. But you insisted that you didn't forget. About the moon, and the wine, and how very romantic it all was. And you told me that you wouldn't be able to resist me."

"I never said that," said Camille. "I've never used the word resist in my life."

"And then you poked your scrawny finger at me and told me, well, you started to tell me something, but you were too…"

"Drunk?" she asked.

"I was going to say captivating."

"Wow, a big word for you," said Camille.

"Right." Michael laughed. "You put me in my place, that's for sure."

"I certainly did," said Camille.

"But I recall one more thing," said Michael.

"And what's that?"

"I remember you leaning in close and tapping my lips. Like this." He demonstrated on her lips. "Then you demanded I kiss you."

"I never," said Camille. "And I never will. Girls from New Orleans never demand any such thing."

"Is that right?"

"Damn straight," she said.

"Cranky and demanding when you're hot, tough and brave when you're challenged, and spunky and adorable when you're drunk," said Michael. "No wonder I fell for you."

"That's right," said Camille. "You fell for me. And don't you ever forget it."

He snorted a chuckle. "I won't, my sweet."

Michael peered up at the yellow-orange moon, just as he had done in that castle garden. It had been just days ago, but the feeling he was feeling seemed to him it had been there his whole life. He knew it had changed him forever.

Michael exhaled. "That moon really is beautiful. Have you looked?"

"I've looked. I've looked," said Camille.

She peeked up again and then she shook her head. "Damned full moon," she said. "What is it with this country? Is there a full moon every night?"

Michael laughed. "Maybe there is," he said. "I think it should be that way." Then he wiggled his eyebrows. "You see, moonlight is one of Italy's best features. And Rome is Italy's best city. That means Rome in moonlight is its best time."

"You don't say," said Camille. Then she whispered to one side, "A girl doesn't stand a chance in Italy."

Michael smirked. "Of course," he said. "It's at its brightest and it has the most power."

"I'll remember that," said Camille.

"Good," said Michael. "You might need it one day.

Camille smiled warmly at him. Michael combed his hair with his fingers. "You know, my pet," he said, "without you, none of this would have been possible."

"Whatever do you mean?" she asked.

"You know *exactly* what I mean," said Michael. "Without you, I would never have found out Fabio was my half-brother."

"Yes, you would," said Camille. "Fabio was the one who came to tell you, at the square. Don't you remember?"

"Sure. But it was because of you that I let him explain," said Michael.

"Because of me?"

"Exactly," said Michael. "You were the one who convinced me to forgive him. You were the one who made me realize that little fights don't matter and the real thing that's important is that we share our life with the ones we love."

"I did all that?"

"You did," said Michael. He took the final step and was standing right in front of her. "And I just realized that I can't let you go."

"You can't?" she asked.

"No."

"But I must go back to Claude," she said. "I really should. But—"

"I know," he said. "You feel like you owe it to him." Michael sat on the bench and looked into her eyes. "But I can't let you go. Not to Paris. Not to Claude. Not to anyone," said Michael. "You mean too much to me."

Camille shook her head but said nothing.

Michael took her hand in his. "You know, Caterina, she's lovely."

"I know," said Camille. "So warm and so full of life."

"And so caring," said Michael. "She reminds me a lot of my own mother."

Camille nodded, and then squeezed his hand. "Your father must have had good taste in women."

"I guess so."

"Better than you," she said.

Michael eyed her. "Better than me?" he asked.

Camille plucked at his leather jacket. "Sure. And I bet he had better taste in clothes too," she said.

"What? What's wrong with my jacket?"

"I mean," she said, tugging on one sleeve, "what were you thinking when you bought it?"

A wily smirk crept up one side of Michael's face. "There's a cute story behind this jacket, my pet," he said. "Someday I'll tell you."

"I know you will, my darling. I know you will."

He chuckled, and then said, "Let's just drop everything and change our lives. What do you say?"

"Agreed." She cackled. And he loved it.

They looked into each other's eyes. Michael tugged softly on Camille's elbows. She pulled back ever so slightly. Then he wiggled his fingers on both hands tenderly tickling her elbows. She smiled and inched closer to him.

"You know what's going to happen next. Right, my darling?" said Camille.

"I have a pretty good idea," said Michael.

He put his arms around her back and pulled her torso up against his. Michael touched his lips to hers once very quickly and then pulled away. Camille's lips fluttered like the wings of a butterfly in deep summer. Then she pressed them hard against his. And they stayed that way for a long silent moment.

They backed their heads away from each other's and breathed in and out with relief and assurance. And promise for the future.

Then Michael said, "Let's go around the world. Together."

"All right," said Camille, "together. Where shall we start?"

"Anywhere but Paris."

Camille looked at the bottle still in Michael's hand. "Are you going to hold that bottle all night? Or are you going to drink?"

"I think I'll have a drink," he said.

"Hand it over," said Camille. "Ladies first."

"Yes, my pet."

Epilogue

FABIO VITALE DID NOT KNOCK. HE NEVER knocked. He forced his way into Michael's room, which for many years, had been set aside for Michael and Camille whenever they visited Italy. Though it was now called the Boutique Hotel Campo de' Fiori, and Fabio was the owner, the couple from New York never stayed in any other room. The number sign on the door, which read 207, was the only sign in the hotel that did not match the others, because it had come from the original hotel. Fabio didn't often flaunt nostalgia or memory, but kept this particular one close to his heart.

"Michele!" said Fabio, as he made his way into the lavish suite.

Michael was in a light grey suit and was lying on the bed staring up at the ceiling. He very much resembled the Michael of 1977, but had thinning white hair. "What is it?" he said.

"You cannot be glum today, *mio fratello*," said Fabio, walking over to the bed.

"Who said I was glum?"

Fabio rapped the bottom of one of Michael's shoes. "Come on, get up," he said. "Cara is waiting for you."

"Who?"

"Don't tell me you forgot why you're here, in Italia."

Michael sat up on the bed. "I thought I was here for you," he said, smirking.

"You are always here for me," said Fabio, "but this time for Cara, too. She has been planning this big wedding celebration for her daughter. And for the memory of Angelina and Marcello."

"I know, I know," said Michael. "They would have been very proud of both granddaughter and great-granddaughter."

"Then let's go, *andiamo*," said Fabio, "Camilla is downstairs already. She is in her red dress, and she is far too beautiful to not get snatched up by another man. We wouldn't want that, would we?"

"No, we wouldn't, my friend."

"Camilla, she is far too beautiful for you, too, Michele," said Fabio, "you must admit."

"Tell me something I don't know, *mio fratello*."

"Come on," said Fabio, tapping Michael's knee, "*andiamo*."

ANGELINA'S PASTA ALL' AMATRICIANA

THOUGH IT WAS NOT EASY, AND EVEN TOOK some begging, the author convinced Chiara Fortunata to share her grandmother's recipe. Chiara told him that her grandmother did not cook with recipes, but by instinct. So Chiara penned the only ever paper copy of the recipe for her grandmother's legendary pasta all' amatriciana. In exchange for a couple of cases of Chianti Classico Riserva, of course. "You can never have enough Chianti on hand," Chiara told the author. Exactly what he imagined Angelina would say.

INGREDIENTS

Extra-virgin olive oil

150 grams pancetta, diced

1 onion, chopped

2 cloves garlic, chopped

Sprinkle red pepper flakes

1 spoonful tomato paste

800 grams San Marzano tomatoes, puréed

Salt and freshly ground pepper

110 grams grated aged pecorino cheese, plus more for serving

500 grams bucatini or spaghetti, cooked until al dente

DIRECTIONS

1. Heat the olive oil over medium-high heat in a large skillet. Add the pancetta and sauté until golden brown. Let yourself dance in the deliciousness; pancetta makes everything happy.

2. Add onion and sauté until soft. Make a well in center of onion and add garlic and red pepper and cook only until fragrant. Knowing timing is imperative, you don't want to wait forever. Mix everything together.

3. Add tomato paste and mix. It will bring out the sweetness of the tomato, which is vital to enhance the romance in the sauce. Add tomato purée, salt and peeper, and cook for about 15 minutes.

4. Mix in the cheese. Add the pasta and coat with sauce, a perfect marriage.

5. Plate the mixture, sprinkle with extra cheese and serve. Eat it immediately and taste the true meaning of life.

A VERY, VERY BRIEF HISTORY OF CHIANTI WINES & THE LEGEND OF THE GALLO NERO

CHIANTI IS THE MAIN WINE REGION OF Tuscany. It encompasses roughly 7,140 hectares (17,800 acres) of vineyards and exports wines all around the world. The native grape is Sangiovese, Italy's most planted grape. For a wine to be called Chianti, it must be produced with at least 70% Sangiovese grapes. Sangiovese's high acidity allows the wine to match well with all kinds of spicy foods. It's one of the few wines that will not get lost when paired with tomato sauce. "*Certo!*" said Angelina.

In 1716, the Grand Duke of Tuscany, Cosimo III de' Medici, established that the wines produced in three areas of Chianti – Castellina, Gaiole, Radda – should be called "Chianti wines." And so, the first wine region was officially defined. This original area would eventually become the Chianti Classico sub-region. (Today it also includes Greve.) The Chianti Classico sub-region is considered to be the heart and birthplace of Tuscan winemaking. Located between Florence and Siena, this region was traditionally where the fullest, richest wine was produced. In 1932, the term "Classico" was added, to distinguish it from the wine produced outside the territory delimited by Cosimo III.

CHIANTI

Chianti wines (without the other classifications) are usually aged for about 6 months. Chianti is a young, simple and tart wine with high acidity. It has savory flavors and pairs well with richer fatty dishes such as the slow-simmered *Ragù al Chingiale*, which is made with wild boar, *Bistecca alla Fiorentina* and pizza!

CHIANTI CLASSICO

Chianti Classico wines are premium Chianti wines that tend to be medium-bodied with firm tannins and medium-high acidity. The primary notes associated with Chianti wines are black and red fruits, like plum, blackberry, cherry, black cherry and red currant. The Chianti Classico wines are more suitable for aging than Chianti wines. They require a one-year period of aging in oak barrels before they can hit the market.

CHIANTI CLASSICO RISERVA

One step beyond is Chianti Classico *Riserva*, which must be aged at least 2 years. Its savory notes, elegance, and aptness for food pairing make it an impressive bottle to bring to any dinner party. Even a party for two relaxing on a stone bench in a garden under the moonlight in Rome.

Cosimo III knew good wine. He showed us where to look for Tuscany's best. You'll always know you found a true

Chianti Classico by the legendary black rooster on the neck of the bottle.

Why a black rooster? Read on to find out why.

The *Gallo Nero* (Black Rooster) has become the trademark symbol for Chianti Classico wines. It represents a consortium of producers that banded together to protect authentic Chianti wines. They adopted the *Gallo Nero* to represent their consortium and to symbolize their commitment to quality and Chianti integrity.

The origins of the symbol are linked to an ancient folk legend, which tells how the political boundaries of the Chianti hills were defined. During the Middle Ages, the Republic of Florence and the Republic of Siena competed for supremacy over the Chianti region. Florence and Siena had long been enemies, and this region was for a long time the subject of continuous and violent clashes.

The two cities wished for the conflicts to come to an end. So they decided on a very curious and unique system to resolve the issue. At dawn, two knights would leave – one from Siena and one from Florence – in the direction of the Chianti territory. The two powers agreed to draw the border at the exact point where the two men would meet. Obviously, the moment of departure was crucial. Thus, it was decided that both parties would rely on the cockcrow to start the competition. The men of Siena chose a white rooster and fed it well in the belief that it would sing much louder at dawn. But the Florentines had a different idea. They preferred a black rooster. They let their rooster starve for several days and kept him locked in a dark room.

Finally, the day of the competition arrived. Starved by hunger, the black rooster began to sing as soon as he was freed. Hearing the loud song, the Florentine knight was able to leave first, even before the sun came up. In Siena, however, the white rooster, who was full and content, slept a few more hours than his black counterpart and sang at the first light of dawn. Because of this, the knight from Siena left much later than the knight already on his way from Florence. The two knights met at a place called Fonteruoli, which is only 12 km from Siena. That became the border, and almost the entire Chianti region was annexed to the Republic of Florence. What do you know about that.

ABOUT THE AUTHOR

JOSEPH CHIBA WAS BORN AND RAISED IN Queens, where he shared a railroad apartment with his New York-Italian family. At the early age of five, he became fixated on the dream of traveling to exotic locations around the world. After college and a stint teaching English in Japan, he disembarked unto island life in Hawaii. Sipping Mai Tais under a centuries-old banyan tree in the Tropics, he scribbled away on his first book. Together with co-author, Sally Kigasawa, he wrote the novel *Ghava's Island* (2018), a spiritual fantasy adventure that takes place on the mysterious Dowsha Island in an altered dimension.

Prompted by a reunion with his long-lost cousins from Naples, he began to probe into the long and captivating history of Italy. Longing to bite into a true *Pizza Margherita*, witness Michelangelo's most beloved ceiling and hear *"Buongiorno"* for himself, he made a series of trips to Italy which formed the basis for his second book, *Rome in Moonlight.*

A history buff with a curious mind, he travels to set his thoughts free from everyday life and allow his imagination to paint the pictures of the worlds he envisions.

Never admitting that this is his home, he lives in Manhattan with his wife.

Made in the USA
Coppell, TX
14 January 2021

48164272R00171